"I'm g[oing] Lingeri[e]"

"Max!" Ari protested in a whisper as he made his way to a large basket filled with colorful scraps of silk.

Max examined the wispy undergarments as if he was combing through his fishing net. "What size?"

She knew he'd badger her until he found out, so she said, "Six."

"Good." He held up a pair of white bikini panties that were ninety-nine percent lace. "What do you think?"

"They're not very practical."

With a wicked grin, Max said, "I'm not interested in practicality," and headed toward the cashier.

Unwilling to face the salesclerk's amusement, Ari fled the store. Max joined her a few minutes later, his purchase tucked under his arm.

"I don't know what you're going to do with that underwear," Arianna said mulishly.

"I do," Max said softly. He handed her the package, his eyes challenging her. "Someday, I'm going to take them off you."

"What would *I* do if I went to the wrong wedding?" **Kristine Rolofson** asked herself after reading about the proper etiquette of such an act in "Miss Manners." And she had the genesis of a wonderful romance. Prolific and popular—this is her fifth book—Kristine has been busy with her children, her husband and moving house. Of course, Kristine likes to do things efficiently. She and her husband bought a new, portable house and had it delivered—completely furnished. All she had to do was plug in her computer and get to work on her next Temptation novel!

Books by Kristine Rolofson

HARLEQUIN TEMPTATION
179—ONE OF THE FAMILY
259—STUCK ON YOU
290—BOUND FOR BLISS
323—SOMEBODY'S HERO

The Last Great Affair

KRISTINE ROLOFSON

Harlequin Books

TORONTO • NEW YORK • LONDON
AMSTERDAM • PARIS • SYDNEY • HAMBURG
STOCKHOLM • ATHENS • TOKYO • MILAN

With love and thanks to Neringa Bryant,
who encouraged this story and gave me a chance
to be a bridesmaid once again

Published May 1991

ISBN 0-373-25448-1

THE LAST GREAT AFFAIR

1

MAXIMILIAN COLE watched his best friend pace back and forth across the tiled floor of the chancel. At this rate the groom would wear himself out before the ceremony began. "Don't you think you should calm down?"

Jerry glanced up and shot him a worried look. "My ass is in a sling if this doesn't go well."

"Maybe you'll luck out." Heedless of wrinkling the white tuxedo jacket, Max shoved his hands into his pants pockets. He stood nearly a head taller than his friend, and although the two men were the same age, they couldn't have appeared more different. Jerry's red crew cut and freckles gave him a boyish air. Max looked thirty-nine; half a lifetime at sea had weathered his skin to an attractive, rugged texture. His thick, dark hair tumbled onto his forehead, and the customary twinkle in his sea-blue eyes intensified at the sight of Jerry's discomfort.

The groom looked at his watch. "In three minutes Barb is going to walk down that aisle."

"That's right." Max's voice was mild. "That's why we're all here today. To see you two joined in holy wedlock."

"This is no time for sarcasm, Max. Are you sure you haven't seen her come in?"

Max knew they were no longer talking about the bride. "I don't even know what she looks like."

"Short," Jerry said. "Dark hair, brown eyes." He fingered his collar as if trying to get more air. "She likes big earrings."

Max walked over to the altar and surveyed the crowd of wedding guests. A low murmur of conversation hummed beneath the organ music while the ushers continued to escort guests to their seats. Huge cascades of white flowers decorated the head of every pew and pale June sunshine filtered through the stained-glass windows. Quite a production, he thought, examining the rows of wedding guests. There was an amazing number of women seated in the crowd; it was as if something about a marriage drew them like a magnet.

Then he saw her, a tiny woman in a pale peach dress, on the arm of one of Jerry's younger brothers, the skinny kid with the big feet. Max stared as she slipped into her seat. Clusters of pearl earrings dangled to the woman's shoulders, and sable hair curled from under the wide-brimmed hat. Was this fragile-looking person the troublemaker Jerry had described?

Max stepped back and rejoined his perspiring friend. "It's possible," he said. "Groom's side, thirteenth row."

"Damn," Jerry groaned. "What am I going to do?"

"You got yourself into this, buddy. And I think it stinks." He clapped Jerry on the shoulder. "If it's any reassurance, there are at least sixty women out there, and I'll bet they're all wearing earrings."

"This is no time for jokes." Jerry groaned again. "You're supposed to be my best man."

"I'm your friend, not your priest."

Jerry paid no attention, trying to see the crowd from his hiding place behind a tall arrangement of pink chrysanthemums. "I can't see."

"She's the one wearing a white hat."

Jerry turned toward Max. "You've got to get her out of here."

"No way." He'd never hustled a woman out of church before and he wasn't going to start today.

"C'mon, man . . ."

Max stood firm. A big man, he wasn't easily pushed around—physically or in any other way. "You don't even know if it's her. You don't even know if she means trouble."

"She does," Jerry said, fingering his collar again. "She's been trouble from the first day I met her and she always will be."

Max once again tried to be reasonable. "Maybe, maybe not. Get hold of yourself."

Jerry jumped as the first chords of the processional filled the church. "Watch her, Max. Let me know if she moves."

"And if she does?"

"Get her out of here."

"All right," Max said with a sigh, catching the priest's motion to come forward. He took Jerry's elbow and aimed him toward the altar. "Let's go greet your bride."

ARIANNA EXCUSED HERSELF as she stepped past the other occupants of the pew. An old woman glared at her as if she expected Ari to usurp the coveted aisle position. Ari didn't blame her. The lady looked as if she'd been sitting in that seat for three days waiting for the wedding to begin.

Ari sat down on the hard wooden pew as the organ music stopped. She watched an usher escort an older woman, probably the groom's mother, to her seat in front. As the organist played the chords to announce the bridesmaids, Ari smoothed the tiny pleats of her narrow skirt and obediently stood to face the aisle. She hated to be late, but had snagged one of the legs of her cream-colored panty hose at the last minute; now there was a stiff glob of nail polish stuck to her right thigh.

Ari discreetly looked around the crowd for someone she recognized, but it was hopeless. Seven years made a huge difference—aunts and uncles aged, and cousins grew up. The usher had also escorted her to the groom's side of the church, probably to even up the rows. Why had she let her mother con her into attending? Just because Mom had been embroiled in one of her twenty-seven different varieties of domestic emergencies with her grandsons didn't mean Ari should have been coerced to take her place at this wedding. *My own fault*, she decided. *I should have come up with an excuse faster.*

"Weddings," her mother had insisted, "are so lovely and inspirational."

Inspirational like hell, Ari thought. She frowned, then tried to look as if she were having a good time. Tried to look pleasant instead of disagreeable. It was a stretch.

Ari looked past the elderly couple and saw a lavender-gowned bridesmaid step nervously down the aisle. She looked as if she was barely out of high school, and Ari suddenly felt twice as old as her thirty-two years. The parade of bridesmaids passed slowly by, then the chords of the wedding march resounded. *Great*, she thought. *Now Uncle Harry will walk one of his six daughters down the aisle and give her away to what's his name.*

Ari stared as the bride and her father came into view. It wasn't Uncle Harry. Unless Harry had lost two hundred pounds and grown hair. Mom had described cousin Effie as "healthy." The young woman behind the veil had no waist to speak of and even in heels was shorter than herself.

The wrong place at the wrong time. Is this the story of my life or what? Ari looked around, hoping she would finally recognize someone, but even as she scanned the rows of backs in front of her she knew it was hopeless. Never mind that she was positive she was supposed to be at Saint Catherine's at two o'clock on Saturday, June 23. It couldn't possibly be polite to watch strangers get married. Ari looked at the empty pew to her right and noted the escape route if offered. Was it possible to tiptoe out before anyone noticed? Even more important, could she get away with it?

She quickly assessed the situation. The music was mercifully slow. The bride's small steps, Ari assumed, would add to the time it took to make it to the altar. The church was crowded, at least the first two-thirds of it, and everyone else was looking at the bride, anyway. No one could possibly care if she slipped from the pew to the side aisle and then quietly out the door.

Her decision made, Ari clutched her small bag in one hand and edged sideways, making sure her heels didn't touch the floor. She'd pick up the pace once she hit the aisle, maybe even try to look sick instead of embarrassed in case anyone noticed her departure.

Someone had. A tall, dark-haired man in a white tuxedo stood blocking her path as if he'd been waiting for her.

"Ex—" Ari began in a whisper, but he cut her off.

"Oh, no, you don't," he said.

Ari glanced up at him, noting wavy hair and strong, tanned features before looking away. One of the best-

looking men she'd ever seen in her life didn't want her
to leave the church? Nothing was making any sense today. She tried again, stepping into the aisle.

"Excuse me."

"*This* way," he ordered, keeping his voice low. He
touched her elbow, as if to guide her away from the altar. Why would he think she wanted to head in the
wrong direction?

Ari stared into cold blue eyes fringed with black
lashes. The old cliché "ruggedly handsome" popped
into her head. His mouth tightened when she hesitated, and the grip on her arm increased.

"All right," she murmured, letting him escort her.
Though she didn't seem to have any choice in the matter, she hoped he knew of a door that would open quietly and let her out into the sunshine. He was obviously
a member of the wedding party; a crisp white carna-
tion decorated his lapel. "You don't have to do this," she
whispered to his chest. "I can find my own way out."

There was no answer, just the steady pressure of his
large hand on her upper arm. The organ music had
stopped, and a hush fell over the crowd just as Ari's escort pushed her into the vestibule. He hesitated near the
closed double doors, then tugged her into a small room
to the left.

"Side door," he muttered. "No noise."

"Fine with me," Ari replied. "You can let go of my
arm now."

"Not a chance."

Ari sighed and let him lead her through the small
room. She told herself she should be used to masterful,
outdoorsy men. Montana was full of them, but few
wore white tuxedos and none of the men she'd dated

had ever hauled her out of a building. Rhode Island was more interesting than she remembered.

She stepped carefully over a cardboard box full of pamphlets, then watched her escort twist the door's brass knob. Minutes later they stood on the soft green lawn of Saint Catherine's Chapel by the Sea, and the man finally released Ari's arm.

"Look," he said, staring down at her. He hesitated for a moment, then continued. "I don't know what kind of game you're playing here, but don't think for a minute that you're going to get away with it."

His voice was deep and resonant, the kind that would carry for miles, Ari decided. The words made no sense, though. "Game?" she echoed blankly.

"Lady, you can't go messing around in people's lives."

"This is a little confusing. I don't think I'm the person you think I am," Ari explained.

"Don't try to con me. It won't work."

"I'm sorry," she said simply, taking a step backward. She would humor him, she decided. Play along until she could make a run for it. "I seem to have made a mistake."

"Jerry did, too. A big one, but that doesn't mean he has to pay for the rest of his life."

"Jerry?"

The lips tightened again, grooves edging the sides of his mouth. He was even great looking when he frowned.

"Don't play dumb, honey. Save the act for someone who cares."

Ari hung on to her temper. *Humor him, remember?* She edged toward the sidewalk, hoping she could get around him and to the parking lot on the other side of the building. "You're absolutely right. Uh, Jerry, should get on with his life now."

"Lady, just promise me you won't go back in there."

Arianna nodded solemnly, making a small X motion near her lace lapel. "Cross my heart." She had no intention of trying to figure out where her cousin and Uncle Harry were walking down the aisle, so entering any more churches today was out of the question.

The muffled sound of organ music filled the air, and Max looked guiltily toward the building. He should be standing next to Jerry, doing his duty as best man, instead of guarding the doors of the church. It was a good thing he'd thought to slip the wedding ring to Jerry's brother before he rushed down the aisle to block the woman's path to the altar.

"I'd better let you get back to the wedding," the strange woman told him, stepping across the grass and onto the sidewalk as if she didn't have a care in the world. He was willing to let her go, but didn't especially like the direction she was headed in.

"Stay away from the church," he growled.

She stopped, turning wide brown eyes in his direction. The hat enchanted him. Its wide brim framed her delicate features and highlighted her ivory complexion. The picture of innocence, he thought, almost willing to believe he might have made a mistake. Then she swore at him.

"What?" He caught up with her, but still couldn't believe he'd heard that particular phrase from such a demure-looking female.

"You heard me. Which word did you have trouble with? 'You' or—?"

"Funny you should suggest it," he interrupted, holding her gaze.

Her eyes flashed, then she smiled. "You'll have to excuse my temper. I made a simple mistake this afternoon, and I'm through being bullied. I'm going to—"

"No," Max said, grabbing her hand. He was a man used to making quick decisions, and this situation called for action. "You're coming with me. The only thing worse than ruining the wedding would be crashing the reception." *Or the honeymoon.* Max figured anything was possible. He tugged her along the sidewalk, toward the docks of Galilee.

"I don't intend to ruin anything," she protested. "I only thought I'd go to the library on my way home."

He could almost believe it. She looked more like an old-fashioned librarian than the experienced seductress who'd tried to blackmail Jerry into marrying him. "The library. Nice touch."

"Could you slow down? This is a narrow skirt."

"Okay." It was a reasonable request, especially since Max didn't have the faintest idea of where he was taking her. He shortened his steps, but kept her small hand tucked inside his.

"Thank you." Ari began to doubt her own sanity. Did she have an evil twin? The thought almost made her laugh out loud. Growing up as the only girl with five brothers had made her long for a sister, evil or otherwise. But besides being able to swear like a sailor, she'd also learned how to defend herself, so that if at any time this particular man grew dangerous, Ari knew exactly what to do. Neither his private parts nor his Adam's apple were safe. For now, though, the clasp of her hand inside his rough one remained gentle.

The smell of the ocean grew stronger as they approached the busy section of the only commercial fishing village in Rhode Island, the third largest in New

England. Tourists strolled along the wide one-way street that paralleled the Harbor of Refuge. Behind the packing plants, restaurants and fresh fish stores lay the docks.

Max hesitated, then carefully led "the librarian," as he had started thinking of her, across the street toward a large white building. The simple sign read Cole Products, Inc., but Max barely looked at it. One glance through the alley told him what he wanted to know: his newest acquisition, *Lady Million*, was still at sea. That was bad news—the boat hadn't hit schools of money fish in days and would have to stay out until it did. What a life! Still, he would've been with the crew if it hadn't been for the wedding. Max took a deep breath and filled his lungs with the ocean air.

"If you think you're hauling me into that alley, you've got another thing coming," the librarian said softly.

He looked down at her, but all he could see beyond the top of her hat was that her high heels were dug into the sandy parking area. "I'm the best man, not a rapist."

She tilted her head back, and Max looked into those clear brown eyes again. "And I'm not whoever you think I am," she said.

"I can't take the chance."

"So, now what?"

"We act like tourists," he suggested, guiding her along the sidewalk. "See? People are smiling at us."

"Because we're a bit overdressed."

They passed the open door of the Beach Shed, and Max inhaled the smell of frying clam cakes. "We have some time to kill. Are you hungry?"

"Forget killing time. You could take me back to my car," she suggested. "You could let me go home."

He could, Max knew. He could return to the church, stand in the receiving line at the reception, drink cheap champagne and dance with the bride's sister, a seventeen-year-old bridesmaid who followed him around like a little puppy. He could nervously check all entrances to the enormous country club in the hope that the librarian wouldn't reappear. He could drink too much and go home alone. Again.

Or, Max thought, watching the huge Block Island ferry deposit a hoard of passengers on the mainland, he and his little friend could go to sea. With his free hand he tugged at his tie and loosened the collar of his shirt.

"WE'RE GOING to Block Island?" Ari couldn't believe it.

He released her hand to tug his wallet from his inside jacket pocket and pulled several bills from its thick folds. "That's right."

Ari hesitated. She could make a run for it or make a scene and scream for a policeman. She could go home to the typically chaotic Simone household, where she'd either end up babysitting her nephews or cutting potatoes into neat little cubes for chowder. The best she could hope for would be the chance to reread *Pride and Prejudice*.

"For a supposedly innocent woman, you're not struggling very hard," he said, reaching to clasp her hand again.

"I'm having fun," she answered. *Crazy but true.* She was free. No one would expect her home for hours, and it was a beautiful day. Why shouldn't she be having fun? Ari continued to stand in the line of casually dressed summer visitors; surely someone would help her if she chose to ask for help? She glanced up at the solid shoulders of the best man. He was at least five years older than her, probably about her brother Kevin's age. For some crazy reason she couldn't explain, she almost liked him. She *did* like him. "Why are we going to Block Island?"

He shrugged. "I need some air."

Ari hung on to her hat as the breeze whipped around them. "Well, this ought to do it."

He smiled down at her. An utterly devastating smile, Ari noted. Warmth finally highlighted those deep blue eyes of his. "You'll have a good time."

"What if I get seasick?"

"You won't." He looked toward the horizon. "It's pretty calm for June, despite the clouds."

"I haven't been to Block Island since I was thirteen. It was a seventh-grade field trip and everyone on the ferry threw up."

"Including you?" He waved to the teenage boy in charge of one of the huge rope coils. Ari watched the kid's face light up.

"Yes," she said. "You live around here?"

He nodded. "This is my home."

The way he said it made Ari pause before asking, "Galilee or the Atlantic Ocean?"

"Both, I guess." He released her hand to touch her back, then guided her through the crowd, making Ari feel as if this was becoming more of a date than a mild form of kidnapping. He steered her to the stairway, past tourists holding on to small children, bicycles, patio furniture or backpacks. "Let's go topside, where we can see."

Once on the upper deck, they stood in silence along the railing for a few minutes while the ferry roared to life and began its slow journey past the rocky arms of the breakwater and out of the harbor. Ari grew tired of struggling to keep her hat from blowing away while trying not to drop her narrow purse.

He nodded toward the scrap of white satin. "Would you like to put that in my jacket pocket?"

It was such a nuisance she'd like to throw it overboard, but it held her car keys, driver's license, a new tube of lipstick and three dollars. "Well . . ."

"I promise it will be safe. Really."

"Will you hold my hat, please?"

He took the brim between his thumb and index finger.

"Just a minute," Ari said, unsnapping the tiny white envelope and removing the dollar bills. She closed it and watched as he slipped it into his pocket, then turned her back on him while she folded the money into a tiny rectangle and slipped it past the V-necked lace collar into her bra. Hadn't her grandmother tried to teach her it was the only safe place to carry her money? Ari felt about ninety-six years old when she turned back to the railing and faced the man with whom she would spend the rest of the afternoon. "I guess we're still acting like tourists, right?"

"Right. Wave to the people on the breakwater."

Ari did, remembering the hundreds of times she'd sat on the rocks and waved to the festive passengers on the ferry.

"Do you want your hat back?"

She nodded and reached for it. Just then a gust of wind caught the crown and tugged it out of her fingers. Her companion grabbed for it, but the hat danced along the railing, flipped twice and disappeared.

"So much for fashion." Ari smiled at the man's soft curse. "Don't look like that. Losing a hat is not a problem."

"I'll buy you another," he said.

She shook her head, enjoying the way the ocean breeze blew the heavy hair away from her face. "3.99 at Woolworths? Don't bother. I only bought it for the wedding."

The wedding. "It must be over by now." Max studied her face for any sign of pain or regret. Something flickered in her eyes. Was it guilt?

"I suppose it is."

"Jerry never told me your name."

"I don't know yours, either," she countered.

He ignored the hint. "Come on. I have to call you something."

Ari thought of the book she'd left on the nightstand. "Jane," she said. "Jane Austen."

He gave no sign of recognition. "You know," he said, leaning on the railing, "I can't figure out what you hoped to accomplish today. Crashing a wedding is a crazy stunt." *And you don't look the least bit crazy*, he added silently.

She mimicked his pose and turned her face toward his. "I tried to explain, but you wouldn't listen."

"I'm listening now, Jane." Peach silk and lace, high heels and pearl earrings. The entire package had his attention, all right.

A few moments passed, but instead of offering information, she had a question of her own. "Who are you? Besides the best man, I mean."

Max sighed, but couldn't help smiling at her stubborn refusal to be bullied. "Charles. Charles Dickens."

"We make quite a pair, then, don't we?"

"So, Jane, what else do you do besides write books?" He inched closer.

"You caught me," she said and laughed.

"How about the truth?"

"I've been telling you the truth all along, Charles."

"My name is Max."

"Max," she repeated. "Short for—?"

"Maximilian." He wanted to reach out and touch the cluster of pearls that dangled beside the soft skin of her neck, but kept his hands on the boat's railing. Jerry's words of warning echoed through his head, something about this woman meaning trouble from the first day he met her. *Consider yourself warned, Cole, and take your chances.* "Your turn."

"I thought you knew. Didn't, uh, Jerry tell you?"

"No." Jerry had offered few details of his stupidity and Max hadn't asked.

"Ari. Short for Arianna."

"Arianna," he repeated. "It suits you."

"I'll tell my mother you approve."

"Please do," he murmured. "You're obviously from around here."

"Why do you say that?"

"The seventh-grade field trip to Block Island."

Ari had no intention of telling him her last name. He was bound to recognize it if he actually lived near Galilee, as he claimed. This afternoon was turning into quite an adventure; being mistaken for someone who would disrupt a wedding ceremony was bizarre enough, but to be escorted out of the church and hauled onto a ferry was truly a once-in-a-lifetime experience. In a few hours she would have to return to her summer role of dutiful daughter and loving sister, but for now she'd given in to temptation. She would enjoy this afternoon in the company of one of the handsomest men she'd ever seen. "Let's not discuss the past," she said in what she hoped was a mysterious tone.

His eyebrows rose. "All right," he agreed. "Then why don't you tell me what you were going to do after you'd ruined the wedding?"

"After?"

He nodded. "Did you think Jerry would leave with you?"

"Let's not discuss Jerry anymore, either."

Max was more than willing to agree.

"A truce," he said, gazing out over the blue waters of Block Island Sound. Hundreds of pleasure boats shared the waters with the large, crawling ferry. The gray outline of a Russian trawler appeared on the horizon, and the island's distinctive sandy bluffs rose in the distance. He turned away from the view and looked down at the woman beside him. "All right?"

Ari looked uncertain. "What happens when we get to the island?"

I'm not letting you out of my sight. "What would you like to do?"

"We're not exactly dressed for the beach or renting bicycles."

"Are you hungry?"

"We missed the reception."

"That was the general idea."

"You still think I'm a...wedding wrecker." It sounded funny to her now that there was no danger. The ferry was crowded with passengers, and once she docked on the island Ari could easily lose Max the Best Man. If she wanted to. So what if she only had three dollars? She could call her father or one of the boys to pick her up, even if it meant riding on the *Peggy Lou.* That would

be a last resort, Ari decided. She certainly didn't want
to board anything smaller than this miniature tanker
she was on now.

"I'm not sure," Max began slowly. "But you are a
beautiful woman and, despite the strange circumstances, you're spending the afternoon with me."

"I don't have much choice, do I?"

"Oh, you've had a choice all along." He bent closer
so she could hear his words over the strengthening
wind. "You're an intelligent woman, Jane Austen, and
we both know there are any number of ways you could
avoid my company."

2

FOR THE HOUR LEFT of the trip across the bay, Ari leaned against the railing and ignored her companion, although it wasn't easy. Not surprisingly, Max remained next to her. He was right. She was there because she wanted to be. For now. When she didn't want to be anymore, she would walk away. Easy as that.

A truce, Max had said. No problem. Ari was very good at truces.

As the ferry approached the beacon at Old Harbor, Ari saw weathered cottages dotting the island's green hillsides. Enormous white Victorian hotels faced the sound as if waiting to greet the visitors who would spill off the ferry. When the boat finally slid against the dock, Max was the first to speak.

"Well, Arianna?" He held out his hand. "Shall we go?"

She put her hand in his, the contact strangely electric. "Lead on, Mr. Dickens."

He led her down the stairs and along the gangway. Car doors slammed and motors started up on the lower deck. Soon they were past the crowds in the asphalt parking lot.

"I think the island gets more crowded every year. It's not even the summer season yet, and there's plenty going on."

Arianna looked down the busy street filled with quaint stores and old-fashioned buildings. "It doesn't look much different than it did twenty years ago."

"Only more crowded."

"Are we going to walk?" she asked.

"I have a better idea. Let's get a taxi and take a tour around the island."

Ari looked longingly at the shops on Water Street, then turned to Max. "Won't that take a long time? I don't want to miss the boat back to the mainland."

He shook his head. "The island's only seven miles long. And we have the rest of the afternoon."

"Do I have a choice?"

Max chuckled. "How about a compromise?"

"Such as?"

"I'll give you a tour, then we'll walk around town before the trip home."

Ari nodded her agreement, though she suspected compromise didn't come easily to her companion. He acted as if he was used to giving orders rather than obeying them. It only took a moment for Max to hail a nearby taxi. Once they were in the battered yellow cab, the driver eased past the people crossing the street and followed Max's instructions. Ari, realizing it felt good to sit down, eased the white pumps off her feet. She would have liked to find a bathroom where she could remove her panty hose and toss them into the garbage—but first she needed to find a shop and buy a pair of sandals. A pair of three-dollar sandals, she amended. If only she'd brought her charge card. What was the commercial? Don't Leave Home Without It? Smoothing the skirt of the silk dress, now she knew why.

Max's voice interrupted her thoughts. "Did you know there are supposed to be over five hundred ships sunk in these waters in the seventeen and eighteen hundreds?"

"My father used to tell me sea stories."

Max smiled. "So did mine."

Ari looked out the window at the ocean. "Years ago I read that Captain Kidd dropped off his wife and daughter on Block Island. They spent the winter here while he was off doing whatever pirates did. It was right before he was tricked into giving himself up in Boston."

"Who tricked him? His wife?"

Ari shook her head. "Of course not." And then it occurred to her that he might have someone waiting for him at the wedding reception. Why hadn't she thought of it before? "Are you married?"

"No. Never."

Surprise was mixed with relief as she asked, "Then aren't you being a little cynical?"

He grimaced. "I'm not really, you know. This has just been a difficult day."

"No kidding." She rolled down her window halfway, then glanced at Max. "Aren't you warm in that jacket?"

He shook his head. "What was it about Jerry, anyway?"

Ari noted the exasperation in his voice and felt his gaze upon her face. She looked away. "I thought we weren't going to talk about him anymore." If Max discovered she wasn't a threat to the wedding, he might take her home on the next boat. She wasn't ready to go home and make a million explanations about why she'd missed Effie's wedding. Unless she could manage to fake a description of the ceremony.

"True," he said, stretching his arm along the back of the seat, disturbingly close to Ari's neck.

They rode in silence for a few minutes until Max asked, "Did your father ever tell you the story of the Palatine Light, Arianna?"

The graying cabdriver glanced over his shoulder. "Now don't go tellin' the lady that piece of drivel."

Ari leaned forward. "Why not? I don't remember much about it."

He snorted. "It's a load of garbage, as far as the islanders are concerned, and we've had to listen to it for over a century now."

Max raised his voice so the man could hear. "I'll tell the real story."

The driver nodded and settled a pipe between his teeth. "You'd be best off to look at the bluffs. I'll pull off here, by the Southeast Light, and wait for you while you do."

Ari quickly slipped her shoes on as Max climbed out of the car and turned to give her his hand. She stepped into the strong breeze and watched the waves pound below.

"Wind's coming up," Max said, looking at the sky. "Could be a storm brewing."

Ari's stomach tightened in dread. This was what she hated about the coast, what made her long for the protection of the Rockies. She should have stayed where she was, instead of tempting fate with a return to Rhode Island. "How will we get back?"

"What's the matter?" Max took a step closer and touched her shoulder. "Are you afraid of a little wind?"

Yes! Ari wanted to scream. *I'm afraid of rough water and gales and boats!* Instead she forced herself to sound natural. "I'm not crazy about storms."

"Come on," he said, taking her elbow. "Let's go back to the car. I'll tell you the story of the Palatine Light over dinner." He smiled but his eyes were concerned. "I don't think you want to hear any shipwreck stories right now."

"Dinner?" she echoed.

"I owe you a meal, don't I?" He glanced at his watch. "It's four-thirty. We'll spend another hour sightseeing."

Ari let him tuck her into the cab. She felt safer out of the wind. "Okay, Max. Lead on."

The driver started the engine and drove along the coastline, then inland to the part of the island dotted with colonial farmhouses and small ponds. He showed them Great Salt Pond, the home of many sailboats and races, and took them to see the white clapboard coast guard station before heading back to Old Harbor.

"The fog bank's coming in," the driver warned. "Do you want to drive to Sandy Point?"

"Not this time, thanks," Max said.

Ari remembered her father cursing the unpredictable June fogs. He'd rant and rave, then finally accept the inevitable and, if there was money to spare, take the family to the movies. Ari stood beside Max as he paid the driver. Her spirit of adventure sagged. "Maybe we should take the next boat back," she suggested.

Max slipped his wallet inside his back pocket and took hold of Ari's hand. "Not yet," he said firmly, tugging her along the street. "You wanted to window-shop."

"I could skip it," she offered. "In fact, I'd be willing to wait over there on the dock so I'd be the first one on the boat."

"Not necessary." He led her toward a gleaming white building edged with window boxes. "Besides, it's still not safe."

"Did you ever think—" Ari panted as she hurried to keep up with him "—that if you'd made a mistake about me, a possibly dangerous woman might be ruining your friend's wedding reception?"

"No." Max stopped in front of the Harborview Inn and gazed down at her tousled head. "As much as I hate to believe it, I think you're precisely the woman I need to keep an eye on."

She desperately wished she had an answer for that. Instead, Ari remained silent as they entered the comfortable-looking lobby and Max spoke to the hostess.

"We don't look like tourists, do we?" Ari muttered, noting the stares from the other diners as the hostess guided them through the dining room to an intimate table for two overlooking the harbor.

He shrugged, then casually pulled out her chair. "I suppose not."

"People are staring."

"You're a beautiful woman. Why shouldn't they look?"

Ari studied Max across the table. Didn't he realize people were staring at him? He looked like a movie star in that white tux. "Don't give me that—"

"Would you care for a cocktail tonight?" asked the waitress. She placed large menus in front of them.

Max leaned forward. "Arianna, what would you like to drink? A glass of white wine?"

She shook her head. "Rum and pineapple juice. Make that a double."

"A double," he echoed, raising his eyebrows. Then he turned to the waitress. "I'll have a scotch, neat."

"I'll be back in a moment to take your order."

"Thank you." He turned his attention back to Arianna. The wind from the bluffs had tossed her hair into

waves around her face, hiding much of the pearl earrings that so entranced him. The troubled expression
in her eyes was disturbing. "Are you worried about the
fog?"

"I'm on an island with a strange man, I have three
dollars and the fog is rolling in. What's there to worry
about?" She rested her chin in her hands. "I don't even
have a hairbrush."

"And you've lost your hat," he added, wanting to
smile. Despite her words, she appeared to be remark-
ably serene—with or without a hairbrush.

"Will you give me my purse, please? I'm going to the
ladies' room." She pushed back her chair and stood
while he fished the purse out of his pocket. "That is,"
Ari added, "unless you have any objection to my leaving you alone for a few minutes."

Max smiled and handed her the purse. "I know you'll
return for your drink."

"You've got that right," she muttered.

He watched her walk through the dining room, back
straight, purse clutched in her hand. The demure lady,
right down to the pale stockings and tiny heels. Could
Jerry have been wrong?

Max didn't care. He hadn't had so much fun in
months. Well, he'd always liked surprises. The waitress set the drinks on the table and Max leaned back and
took a grateful swallow of the scotch.

"Would you like to order now? You have forty-five
minutes until the next boat, sir," the waitress said. "No
one's sure if the eight o'clock will be in."

Perfect, Max decided. This was too good to end. He
pulled his wallet out and handed the young woman his
American Express card. "Do me a favor and book two
rooms for tonight, please."

She hesitated. "You might want to check with the coast guard before you decide to stay over."

Max shook his head. "No. I've made up my mind." He took another sip of his drink and stared out the windows at the empty ferry landing. Arianna might have meant trouble for Jerry, but now she'd met her match.

ARI GLARED into the mirror and raked her fingers through her windblown hair. She'd decided against removing the panty hose, fearing her shoes would give her blisters. The day was almost over anyway, and after dinner they'd be back on the boat, heading home.

She didn't even know his last name. He was the best-looking man she'd ever seen in her whole life and had felt genuinely bad about her hat, even though he'd dragged her onto the damn ferry to begin with. He'd toured the island and told her stories, and was taking her to dinner, treating her as if she was his date for the evening, even though he thought she was some sort of nasty person. She hadn't had a date in four months.

She needed that drink.

When Ari made her way back to the table, Max stood to greet her. Always a gentleman, she wondered? The game was about to end. It was about time to end the entire misunderstanding.

He looked pleased with himself, she noticed. That probably wasn't a good sign. She sat down and sipped her drink, the crushed ice melting against her tongue as the spicy rum blazed a trail down her throat.

"Better now?"

Ari nodded and opened the menu. "I think so."

"Are you ready to order?"

She quickly scanned the entrées. "Everything looks wonderful, but I think I'll have the sautéed scallops."

"Not me. I get my fill of seafood," he said, with a rueful smile. "It's the nature of the business."

"You're a fisherman." Naturally with her luck he would turn out to be a fisherman. Why couldn't he do something safe for a living, like sell shoes or help people figure out their taxes?

"Yes, I suppose you could say that."

The waitress hurried over and handed Max a credit card. "You're all set, Mr. Cole."

Cole. So he had a last name.

"Thanks."

They placed their orders, and the busy waitress left.

"So your last name is Cole." What was familiar about that? Then she remembered. "Like the sign on the building in Galilee."

"It's a processing plant," he explained. "The family business."

She knew about family businesses. And families. "What's all set?"

"Our reservations for tonight."

"Reservations?" she echoed. "Not on your life."

"The fog's rolling in," he continued patiently, "and the late boat may not run. Would you prefer a room here at the Harborview or sleeping on the beach? Which is prohibited, by the way."

Ari stared at him across the table. Relief warred with the realization of the inconvenience of staying overnight with no clothes, toothbrush or comb. "You must be joking."

"Nope."

"Maybe the late boat will run."

"And everyone aboard will suffer a hell of a trip."

Including me. Calling her father or one of the boys to come pick her up would be out of the question, too. "You did say rooms?"

"Plural." He smiled. "Any objection?"

She quickly took another large swallow of her drink. "None, Maximilian Cole. But I think there's something we should get straight right now." She pushed her purse toward him across the linen-covered table.

He picked it up and started to put it into his pocket.

"No," Ari said. "Open it."

Max hesitated, his gaze unwaveringly on Ari's face. "What are you getting at?"

"The truth."

He looked down and unsnapped the satin container, lifted the envelope tab and shook the contents onto the table.

"Your salads," the waitress said, balancing two plates and a basket of bread on a tray. She set Ari's plate in front of her, then paused while Max swept Ari's possessions out of the way.

"Thank you," he murmured, avoiding the waitress's curious look. She eased his salad in front of him, plopped the basket in the middle of the table, then hurried away. Max kept his gaze on Ari. "What am I looking at?"

"My driver's license."

He picked up the rectangular piece of cardboard and examined it. If he was surprised, he didn't show it. "A Montana license. So?"

"You'd make a lousy private eye, you know."

He pushed the salad plate aside with an impatient gesture. "What are you trying to prove?"

"I'm not Jerry's girlfriend or whatever."

"Why couldn't you be? He never told me her name. And you could have had this license for a long time while still living in Rhode Island."

But Ari had an answer for him. "Look at the date the license was renewed."

He moved the paper closer to the candlelight and studied it once again. "You just had it renewed last month."

She nodded. "On my birthday."

"You're thirty-two." He smiled at her. "You look younger."

She let the compliment slide by. "And I live in Bozeman, Montana, have brown hair and brown eyes and weigh one hundred and ten pounds."

He checked the statistics. "Arianna Simone," he read, then looked at her. "Related to the Simone brothers?"

"My brothers."

"I know them. I used to buy lobsters from Kevin and Roscoe when they were hauling traps."

Ari settled the large cloth napkin on her lap and reached for a fork. The salad looked delicious. "They'll probably kill you for this," she announced cheerfully.

"Not if I return you with your virtue intact."

"I didn't know my virtue was at stake here—I thought being kidnapped was my major problem."

He dropped the driver's license on the table. "Consider yourself released."

"Thank you." She sampled the salad, realizing how hungry she was.

Max leaned forward. "What were you doing walking out of the church?"

"I didn't walk out. You hauled me out."

"With good reason, I thought."

"Try your salad. It's delicious."

"You haven't answered me."

"Look," Ari said, resting the fork on her plate and picking up her glass. "I tried quite a few times to tell you who I was, but you didn't want to listen." She was enjoying this. Fitting revenge for being forced to wear panty hose and heels for almost five hours.

"You have my attention now," he growled, downing the rest of his drink in one gulp.

"I went to the wrong wedding."

"How could anyone go to—?" He stopped when he saw her expression. "Go on." He sighed.

"My mother couldn't go, so she conned me into taking her place to represent the family at Effie's wedding." Ari allowed herself a small shrug. "One of us must've mixed up the time. I know for sure I was told to go to Saint Catherine's."

"And when did you realize Effie wasn't getting married?"

"Uncle Harry didn't look like himself."

"Uncle Harry is Effie's father?"

She nodded. "That's right. So I tried to sneak out." She sipped her drink, then put it down. "You look like you're going to start laughing. What's your side of the story?"

"Jerry—the groom—had a brief, uh, fling with another woman when he and his fiancée broke off. When he and Barb got back together again, Jerry regretted the entire affair, but the other woman promised to get even."

"And you thought she'd pull something at the wedding?"

"Jerry did. And you fit the description."

"That's what I thought."

She looked out over the harbor as fuzzy lights began to glow through the fog. "The weather is spooky. I hope everyone's safely home."

"Why do you live in Montana?"

"I like it there. It's Big Sky Country."

"So I've heard." He frowned. "But don't you miss the ocean?"

"No."

Max couldn't figure it out. There must be things she wasn't saying. "How long you lived there?"

"Almost eight years."

The puzzle intensified. He watched as she calmly picked up her possessions and replaced them inside the purse, then tucked it away on her lap. "Why?"

She looked up to meet his questioning gaze. "I work there. I teach English literature at the university."

"Do you always come home for the summer?"

"Not usually." Ari thought longingly of the cabin in the Tetons she'd rented last August. "This summer's different. My parents want to sell their house and move into something smaller. I came home to help."

"You don't sound happy about it."

"I'm used to being on my own."

"You're not married."

"No."

"Good."

She turned surprised brown eyes in his direction. "Are you taking a personal interest?"

He smiled, a slow smile that crinkled the corners of his eyes. "Just checking to see how many outraged men I'd have to fend off tomorrow when I take you home."

"Take me back to my car. It'll be safer."

"I know your brothers. They'll hunt me down."

"You look like a man who can take care of himself."

"You're right."

"I'll need to call home," she said as the waitress returned to take their salad plates and deliver the entrées. "I don't want anyone to worry. They probably think I'm still at the reception."

"Fine. You are safe with me, you know."

Ari looked into his serious blue eyes and knew he spoke the truth. "I know," she said softly, but couldn't resist teasing. "You owe me a toothbrush and toothpaste."

"We'll go shopping after dinner."

Ari looked at the sautéed scallops on the antique plate. The aroma made her stomach growl. Since fresh scallops were scarce in Bozeman, she'd spent the last ten days eating scallops every chance she got.

"Is something wrong with your dinner?" he asked.

She shook her head. "I love scallops. It's the only thing I've missed about Rhode Island."

"I don't get it." He frowned. "What's wrong with Rhode Island?"

Ari couldn't think of how to answer. "Nothing at all," she lied. "I guess I'm just a Western girl at heart."

"I could change your mind." The words surprised him. He hadn't meant it to happen, but the woman was getting to him. He admired her spunk, respected her composure and definitely liked her looks. He was tired of casual summer affairs with women in bikinis. Leathery tans and arrogant attitudes no longer turned him on. He was tired of playing games and going to bars. He wanted to settle down with someone like Arianna. Or, better yet, with the lady herself.

She stared at him, her eyes questioning. "I don't think so," she said softly. Her voice was kind. "I'm only here for a few more weeks."

"It could be enough."

Ari shook her head, and Max once again caught a glimpse of pearls. "Let's change the subject," she suggested. "Aren't you hungry?"

Max looked down at his forgotten steak and picked up his knife and fork. "Starved."

LATER, after coffee and blueberry cheesecake, Max led Arianna to the corner phone in the lobby.

"Call from here, in case your parents need to talk to me."

"They won't," she protested. "I'm not fifteen."

"They're still parents."

Ari sighed, and called home collect. After her mother accepted the charges, Ari attempted to explain what had happened.

Then there was a pause, and Max wished he could hear the other end of the conversation.

Ari spoke again, her hair brushing against the receiver. "I know it sounds crazy, but I met some old friends and we've had dinner and are staying here at the uh, Harborview. We'd planned to take the last boat out, but the fog's socked in." She made a face at Max. "Rogue wave? I thought those were only sea stories." She listened again. "No, I won't. Promise." Again Ari listened. "Maybe. See you in the morning. That's right, Harborview. I left the car at the church parking lot."

Max continued to stand nearby, trying to pretend he wasn't listening. He examined a framed seascape on the wall.

Ari spoke again. "Well, one of them is Max Cole." Pause. "Yes, he is." Pause. "Wait a minute, I'll ask him." She turned to Max. "Did you graduate with Kevin or Russ?"

"Kevin. We played football together."

She turned back to the phone. "Kevin."

Max worried while Ari listened to her mother. He'd like to make a few calls himself, find out if the *Million* had checked in yet. And what the hell was this stuff about the rogue wave?

"For heaven's sake, don't worry about it."

Ari sounded aggravated. Max watched her face. She obviously didn't like being bossed around. Why hadn't she protested when he'd pushed her around all afternoon? Maybe she had needed some air, too.

When Ari finally said goodbye and hung up, Max studied her face once more. "Everything okay?"

"Just fine. She knows you."

He shrugged. "Probably."

"What do you mean probably? She told me to have a wonderful time with Captain Cole."

"Everyone knows Peggy Simone's chowder stand." Max took Ari's hand and led her outside. After all, he still owed her a toothbrush.

"She thinks it's terrific that we're stuck on this island."

He smiled down at her disgruntled expression. "So do I," he said, leading her toward the market. "Cheer up, Ari. You can pick out a hairbrush, too."

"GOOD NIGHT, MAX." Ari stopped in the corridor before stepping across navy-blue carpet to enter the bedroom after the housekeeper.

"Goodnight, Jane Austen." The twinkle in his eyes didn't surprise her. "Are you sure you won't join me downstairs for a nightcap? It's still early."

"I'm sure," Ari said, but she wasn't sure at all. He'd grown entirely too charming since he'd found out who she was.

"I'll meet you downstairs for breakfast at eight-thirty and we'll catch the eleven o'clock boat back to Point Judith."

Still giving orders. "All right."

Looking satisfied, he leaned against the wall and waited while the innkeeper unlocked Ari's door.

"This room has a private bath," the woman said, switching on the light to reveal a cozy bedroom. Old-fashioned rose paper decorated the walls and, near the opened window, a pitcher of fresh daisies sat on a gleaming pine dresser.

"It's beautiful," Ari told her, and the elderly woman left to join Max in the hall. Once alone, Ari tossed her purse and the package from the store onto the oversize brass bed. She kicked off her shoes and, after carefully peeling the nail polish from her leg, wriggled out of her panty hose.

Overnight on the island, Ari mused, had not been what she'd planned for this Saturday. Going to the movies with her sister-in-law would have to wait until tomorrow. Ari padded barefoot across the soft blue carpet and looked out toward the harbor. She couldn't see much now that the fog had rolled in. She doubted if the eight o'clock boat had ever left Point Judith. Max had been right, after all. Clever, too, to arrange for rooms so quickly.

Maximilian Cole, Ari decided as she turned away from the window, was definitely a force to be reckoned with.

3

"SNEAKING OUT AGAIN?"

Ari hesitated on the landing and surveyed the man waiting for her at the bottom of the stairs. Freshly shaved, Max looked as if he'd been awake for hours. He was casually dressed, his white shirt tucked neatly in his slacks, the formal tie and tuxedo jacket nowhere to be seen.

"No," she said, meeting the amusement in his deep blue eyes. "I'm meeting a man for breakfast."

"Two hours early?"

"I needed coffee. Desperately." Ari stepped quickly down the remaining stairs. Max smelled as good as he looked, she noticed, trying not to stand too close to him. A combination of soap and fresh air. "And besides, I'm an early riser."

"Me, too." Max looked at his watch. "It's only seven. We can take an earlier boat back unless I can talk you into seeing the other part of the island."

"I don't think so, thank you." Spending another day with the attractive Captain Cole would be asking for trouble, and Ari didn't relish wearing her rumpled dress any longer than absolutely necessary.

"Another time, then," he said. He guided her toward the dining room. "Come on, then. We'll have breakfast."

"Could I just have some coffee first?" Ari asked weakly, unwilling to face a plate of eggs right away. "Plunging right into a large meal just isn't my style."

"Wait here," he said, leaving her in the hallway.

Another order. But she was too sleepy to argue, and instead walked over to the window to look out over the harbor. The sky was overcast, but the sea didn't appear to be choppy. That was a relief.

"I remembered you like it black."

Ari turned as Max entered the foyer. He offered her one of the white mugs of steaming coffee.

"Thank you." She held the cup carefully so it didn't burn her fingers.

"Come on," he said, gesturing to the door. "There are tables outside if you'd like to sit on the terrace. It's cool, but the sun's trying hard to come out."

"Okay." She followed Max outside to a small round table and sat down across from him on a cushioned metal chair. Ari sipped her coffee and enjoyed the smell of the ocean. The soft murmuring of waves was especially soothing. She'd tossed and turned last night, restless in the dark of the unfamiliar room. Too many strange beds, she decided, thinking of the narrow childhood bed at her parents' home. And last night's firm, wide mattress had lent little comfort. Ari pictured her own water bed and sighed. It was one of the best purchases she'd ever made.

"You're quiet this morning," Max said.

"I don't talk much in the morning. It takes me a while to wake up."

Max smiled, a devilish expression flashing across his handsome face. "I'll remember that."

Ari raised her eyebrows. *You won't have the chance,* she wanted to say, but remained silent. She looked away and sipped her coffee, glad to feel it cooling in the breeze, and took a larger swallow. Thank heavens for caffeine.

He leaned back in his chair. "If you can't talk, will you listen?"

Ari nodded. "Sure."

"Good," he said. "I've had time to think about yesterday. That was a pretty crazy set of circumstances, wasn't it? Don't say anything, Ari—you can just nod yes or shake your head for no."

Ari nodded.

"But it worked out."

She looked down at her wrinkled dress and slipped her bare feet from the confining shoes. "In what way?"

"We met each other." He leaned forward, setting his mug on the table and resting his forearms on the white metal. "You're an intriguing woman."

"Thank you, I think."

He frowned slightly. "I meant it as a compliment, but that's not the point. Are you involved with someone?"

Ari thought of the rancher with whom she'd ended a relationship last year. "No, but—"

"Are you going to be here in Rhode Island long?"

Not if I can help it. Ari shook her head. "Look, Max, I—"

"What else do you do there?"

"Where?"

"In Montana." His voice was edged with impatience.

"I told you last night, I work for the university. Teaching English."

He nodded. "I remember. But what do you do for fun? Are you happy?"

"Isn't this getting a little personal?"

"That's the idea."

Ari took another swallow of coffee. "Of course I'm happy," she said finally. He looked as if he didn't want to believe her. "Why wouldn't I be?"

"Because you grew up here. Don't you miss the ocean? The beach?"

"Right now I miss the mountains, cool mornings and colder nights, camp fires and cowboy boots."

Max picked up his cup and studied her over its rim. "A long sentence. You must have finished your coffee."

She laughed, putting the empty mug on the table-top. "Very observant. Why the third degree?"

"Call it curiosity."

A young waitress appeared with a pot of coffee and refilled their cups. Ari began to feel better now that the caffeine was zipping through her bloodstream and leaned back in her chair, cradling the cup between her hands. A shaft of sunlight broke through the clouds. She studied the handsome man across from her as he thanked the waitress and reserved a table for two.

"We'll eat in about ten minutes," he told her before turning back to Ari. "Enough time?"

It wasn't really, as Ari preferred brunch to breakfast any day, but she guessed Max must be starving. "Fine. Any more questions?"

"Plenty, but they can wait."

Ari decided it might be a good time to change the subject of the conversation. "You never told me your version of the Palatine Light."

"What?" Max smiled at her, a slow grin that crin-kled the corners of his eyes. "You don't want to ask me anything personal—just in the interest of fair play?"

"No, I don't think so," Ari lied. "You're Captain Max Cole and you're in the fishing business in Galilee.

You've never been married and there isn't a whole lot in this world that intimidates you. Am I right?"

Max stood up and held out his hand. "Absolutely. Shall we go eat?"

"All right," Ari said softly, wishing for a brief moment that Max lived in Montana and made his living rounding up cattle instead of fish.

Max wisely kept the conversation impersonal while they enjoyed breakfast together. At least, he thought, he enjoyed it. Arianna didn't eat anything but a slice of white toast smeared with apple jelly. But she managed to drink three more cups of coffee. It was a wonder that woman didn't have a heart attack from all the caffeine.

Despite what she'd said about being an early riser, the woman was not a morning person. But he would forgive her anything if she would share more mornings with him. He didn't stop to question why he was so intrigued—or so certain. Max tried to tell himself he'd been on land too long. A sensible man didn't fall in love overnight. And Max Cole had always thought of himself as a sensible man.

"Are you sure that's all you want to eat?"

Ari smiled as she pushed her small plate to one side. "Yes." She picked up her coffee cup and took another sip. "I'm more of a lunch person," she told him. "It's two hours earlier in Montana, so eating breakfast back East is really hard."

"I'll take you to lunch, then."

She shook her head. "You don't have to buy me any more meals. Just take me to my car."

Max waited for the waitress to clear the plates before answering. He would have liked to take her back upstairs to bed. His bed. He would have made love to her—exquisite, passionate love—until, hours later, she realized they were meant for each other. "What's so special about Montana? Isn't it flat and dry, with a lot of cows?"

"And mountains, clear air, no humidity and space. Open roads."

Max gestured toward the view of the water from the window near their table. "Open water."

Ari didn't look. "We agree to disagree, then."

"It makes life interesting."

"True." She avoided his intense blue gaze and re-folded the heavy linen napkin in her lap. "What time is it?"

He leaned back in his chair and signaled to the waitress. "Time to go," he said with a sigh.

"Stop looking at me as if I was a prize fish you'd pulled up in your net."

His chuckle disarmed her, since she'd expected him to argue about it. "Sorry."

Moments later, after Max had settled the bill and retrieved his tuxedo jacket from his room, he took Ari's hand and led her outside again. The breeze was warm, the sun clearly determined to overwhelm the clouds with its yellow light. Ari didn't mind holding hands with Max. She even liked it. He was gorgeous, had a sense of humor and, despite the disturbing intensity in his eyes when he looked at her, she felt perfectly comfortable walking beside him. Almost comfortable, she amended, realizing that touching his skin created a startling array of physical reactions. Pleasant physical reactions, she amended, but that didn't mean she would drag him into the dunes and strip off all of her clothes and make love....

"What's wrong?"

"Uh, nothing," she said, a bit guiltily. "Why?"

"The death grip you have on my hand."

"Sorry." Ari loosened her fingers.

"If you're nervous about going back on the boat, we can—"

"Oh, no," Ari breathed. Coming toward them near the ferry landing were two very familiar figures. White-hot anger began to seep through her. She stopped and dug her heels into the gravel once again, leaving Max to look down at her face, then across the pavement to the two grinning young men who were sauntering their way.

"They could only be Simones," Max said, noting the curly brown hair and dark eyes. Shoulders like line-backers, which they probably were in high school. Unshaven and bleary-eyed, the young men looked as though they'd spent a good part of Saturday night partying.

Ari nodded grimly. "Jimmy and Joey, the two youngest."

"Hey, airhead!" one of them called. "You need a ride home?"

"Airhead?" Max murmured.

"Their nickname for an older sister who spent hours with her nose stuck in a book."

The young men approached. Ari reluctantly made the introductions, but realized too late that they were unnecessary. The boys were acquainted with Max, although they didn't call him by his first name.

"What are you two doing here?"

"Mom got us up at dawn to come give you and your friends a ride home." Joey yawned, scraping a hand over his rough whiskers. "Don't get mad at me. It wasn't our idea."

"I'll bet not."

Max casually draped an arm around Ari's shoulder.

"Hey!" Joey looked past Ari's shoulder. "Where's everybody else?"

Ari and Max glared at him. Slowly he got the message and hid a grin. "Oh, I get it."

"You get what?" Max asked, a threatening growl in his voice.

"Uh, nothing. I get nothing," the kid stammered quickly. Joey turned to Ari as if pleading for help. "Dad's boat's around the other side of the docks. You want a ride home or what?"

Ari realized Max's arm lay around her shoulders in a disturbingly intimate fashion. He didn't seem concerned by her family's interference, but she was furious. She hadn't wanted a ride home and, at age thirty-two, was perfectly capable of getting there under her own steam. "It's too bad Mom got you up for nothing."

"Aw, Ari . . ."

She turned away. "You'd better go get some coffee."

"Mom's gonna have a fit. You sure you two don't want to come with us?"

Ari looked up at Max. He shook his head. "I'm sure," she said, turning away from her brothers. "I'm going home with the man who brought me."

The return trip across the bay was slightly choppy, and Ari was glad she'd only eaten toast. Max stood at the railing, impervious both to the wind and the slight motion of the huge boat.

There didn't seem to be anything more to say.

Ari wished he'd talk. She loved hearing his low voice. She wished she could close her eyes and listen to him—the gaze from those dark blue eyes was entirely too piercing. He was watching her—she knew it even without looking at him. She turned her back upon the ocean and examined her fellow passengers. No one was paying them the slightest attention, despite her silk dress, Max's fancy white shirt, white pants and shoes. Disreputable, that was the word for it. She hid a smile as she thought of the wedding yesterday.

"I suppose Jerry is off on his honeymoon now," she said.

Max looked uncomfortable and didn't say anything.

"I suppose he thinks you did him a big favor, hustling me out of the church like that."

"Yeah, I'm a real hero."

She pointed out the rocky breakwater. "Home."

"Now what?"

She was puzzled. "I suppose you go home. You do have one, don't you?"

"Yes," he growled. "I'll take you to your car. Or to mine. I'll drive you home."

"No." Her family's interference still stung. She wanted to confront them—her mother—alone.

Max touched her, swinging her around to face him. He tilted her chin with his large, rough thumb and looked down at her as if he couldn't decide what to do next. After a long moment he said, "Have dinner with me tonight."

"You've already asked me that." She softened her refusal, though she knew exploring their attraction to each other would be futile. "I can't."

"Can't or don't want to?"

"Both."

"It's no use, you know." He slid his hand to the side of her face and into her hair. The simple contact sent a jolt of heat through her body, and Ari sucked in her breath. The physical attraction to this man was unbelievable, and she fought to resist it. *Just body stuff,* she told herself. *It's been quite a while since any man has touched me, so it's no wonder I'm a little . . . jumpy.*

"What's no use?"

"Avoiding me." His lips curved into a lopsided smile. "I won't let it happen."

"You don't have any choice," she said. "I'm only visiting here. And I'm not looking for a summer romance."

He frowned. "I outgrew them years ago."

The relief she felt surprised her. "Then we agree."

"You're missing the point." He studied her, as if wanting to kiss her, Ari wondered if he would. She wondered what his mouth would taste like. There would be salt, a touch of the Atlantic spray on his lips and face. And on hers. It wouldn't be a chaste kiss, either. Max Cole didn't play games. He probably liked his women ready and willing, the sex hot and hard and fast. No excuses, no regrets. She watched his eyes darken, then he dropped his hand and stepped away from her.

"I'm simply being honest," she protested, not liking the anger in his face.

"And so am I, Arianna." He turned to the railing and looked at the pleasure boats scattered across the choppy sound. "It's going to be a summer we'll never forget."

"IT CERTAINLY must have been an interesting weekend," Peggy Simone muttered. "Here it is Tuesday already, and you haven't said two words."

"There's not much to say," Ari answered, determined not to give her mother any cause to play matchmaker. *A summer we'll never forget* he'd said. The words had been a promise, not a threat, although the underlying current of sexual awareness remained difficult to ignore. Ari peeled a long strip of brown skin from the potato in her hand, letting the strip fall onto the square of newspaper on the table.

"He's a difficult man to understand," her mother warned. "Not that I wouldn't like to see you settled here."

"Give it up, Mom."

Her mother continued as if she hadn't heard. Peeling potatoes and talking came naturally—the two pleasures went hand in hand as far as Peggy Lou Simone was concerned. Sixty-two, she made it her business to know everything that went on in her family. "To see my only daughter's children, to rock your babies . . . Max Cole would give you many beautiful babies."

"If I wanted them," Ari muttered. Of course she wanted children, but the man she'd intended to marry had been lost at sea. And the romantic dreams of a twenty-year-old had drowned with that high school boyfriend—her first lover, her best friend.

Peggy ignored her once again. "He's also broken a lot of hearts, Arianna."

Ari smiled. "As if your own sons haven't?" The older boys had calmed down now, settled securely with the women they'd decided to let love them, but Joe and Jim continued to cruise the Narragansett bars, partying with their friends at the Neptune in between fishing trips.

Peggy picked up the potatoes and took them to the sink to be rinsed. The kitchen behind the seafood market was all stainless steel, with the huge stove Peggy used to simmer the pots of chowder served to the locals and the tourists.

"They've done their share of catting around, but now look," she continued as if Ari could not help but recognize her logic. "Russ and Karen have five children—five handsome sons," she added with a grandmother's pride. "Kevin and Lin have the two little ones, although how they manage with those two toddlers I'll never know."

"I don't think she planned to have them eleven months apart."

Peggy ignored the comment. "Look at Coe and Ruthie."

"Pregnant with twins doesn't sound too appealing, Mother."

"You only call me Mother when you're being snotty."

"How about Mumsy?"

"Don't be fresh, Arianna Marie. You miss Effie's wedding, spend Saturday night on Block Island with Captain Cole and refuse to let your brothers give you a ride home the next morning. You've peeled potatoes for two days without complaining—"

"Penance," Ari interjected with a slight smile. "I'm paying for my sins."

"So you must have a guilty conscience."

"I didn't sleep with him."

Peggy sighed. "I know that."

"Disappointed?" Ari continued to peel, content with the mindless activity. If it weren't for her mother's curious chatter, she might be able to think. Thinking occupied time, time spent peeling potatoes and mincing fatty squares of salt pork.

Peggy pointed a wet finger at her daughter. "Don't be fresh. Your sex life is your own business."

"Thanks," she said wryly. "I appreciate that."

"But . . ."

Of course her mother couldn't leave it at that, Ari thought. There was no way. She looked up at her and waited.

"I hope you're careful. All I hear on the TV these days, people dying because they didn't protect themselves."

"You're talking to me about condoms?"

Peggy Lou put her hands on her hips. "The same as I do the boys," she said defensively.

"I'm thirty-two."

"So?"

"So I'm old enough to know about safety and condoms and birth control."

"What happened to that farmer you were going with?"

"Rancher," Ari corrected absently.

"Same thing," Peggy said with a shrug.

Ari laughed. Her mother, having lived by the sea all of her life, couldn't imagine men who spent their days away from the sight of water, who dug in the earth and covered waves of prairie instead of ocean. "After three years, we decided we were simply friends, not partners for life."

"No passion, eh?" Peggy sighed, sitting down at the table across from Ari. She picked up a knife and began to attack the potatoes, too. "A very important ingredient, yes?"

Ari thought of Max Cole's green-blue eyes and the intense expression on his face when she'd thought he would kiss her. Her stomach tensed deliciously at the memory and her knife stopped its journey along the curve of the potato.

Peggy studied her daughter's face. "You be careful, my love. You'd better be serious if you tangle with the handsome captain. He'll not let you go so easily like your Montana farmer, you know. He's used to having what he wants, and he works for it, too."

"I'm a big girl, Mom. I can take care of myself." The protest sounded ridiculous, even to Ari's ears. What on earth was she doing making a melodrama out of a simple misunderstanding with a man?

No ordinary man, though, Ari decided, remembering the determined slant to Max's firm mouth yesterday morning when he'd watched her unlock her car door and step inside. He'd stood there on the sidewalk, hands in his pockets, watching as the engine roared to life and Ari backed up, turned and headed for home.

She hadn't looked into her rearview mirror, stubbornly refusing to see if he was watching her manipulate the little car along the near-empty street.

He knew where she lived, or it would be easy for him to find out. There were seventeen Simones in the phone book.

If he wanted her, he could come get her.

THAT WAS EXACTLY what Max planned to do—come get Arianna Simone. Two hundred years ago he could have kidnapped the woman, hauled her off to sea and made her his bride on the slippery wooden deck of a whaling boat before turning toward land. The Block Island ferry had been a damn poor substitute.

Max strode into the dark seafood store, his boots impervious to the wet concrete floor. The bell jangled in greeting, although it had to compete with the rock and roll music blasting from a radio somewhere behind the counter. The place smelled of the sea, thick with salt and tangy. A large lobster tank stood in the corner, and Max absently looked inside at the pegged lobsters slowly crawling on the bottom. He glanced at the nearby board. Good. The price was going up.

He'd given her two days, two long days. He wouldn't wait any longer.

He'd buy a cup of chowder, chat with Peggy and hope to catch Arianna on the premises. If she wasn't there, he could charm Peggy into giving him the information. Of that he was sure.

An obviously pregnant young woman came out of the back room, a stained white apron tied snugly over her rounded belly. "Can I help you today?"

Max didn't recognize her. "Is Peggy around?"

"Sure." She turned and walked slowly to the door. "Mom! Someone to see you!"

Must be one of Ari's brother's wives, Max assumed. The Simones were a fertile bunch. Peggy appeared, wiping her hands on a blue-checked towel.

"Ah," she said, nodding. "I should have known."

"Hi, Peg. I'm looking for Ari," he added unnecessarily.

"You're in luck," Peggy said. "She's in the back, peeling potatoes."

He stepped around the end of the counter and through the door to the back room where Ari was sitting at a large table. Her knife stopped as she looked up at him. Amusement danced in her dark eyes, as if she was trying not to laugh out loud.

"You found me. On purpose or by accident?"

"On purpose," Max said. "I also wanted some chowder."

"To go?" the pregnant woman asked.

"I'll eat it here, thanks." He glanced at Peggy, who was plainly trying hard not to look interested. "Unless anyone has any objections."

Ari thought she could think of a few, but kept quiet while Ruthie scooped soup from the large pot on the stove.

"Have you met my daughter-in-law Ruthie?" Peggy was trying to fill in the silence.

"No," said Max, smiling as Ruthie brought him the bowl of chowder. "I'm very glad to meet you. Which one are you married to?"

"Coe," she answered shyly, using her husband's nickname.

Max nodded. "Tell him I said hello."

"I will," Ruthie answered with a smile.

Max pulled back a metal folding chair and slid into it, setting the bowl in front of him and reaching for the nearby box of plastic spoons.

"Crackers?" Ari suggested, shoving a plastic packet his way.

"Thanks."

He stirred the chowder as if he had all the time in the world, while Ari sat quietly and peeled potatoes. Peggy chopped onions, and Ruthie twisted the long-handled wooden spoon through the pots on the stove. On the radio, Don Henley sang "The End of the Innocence."

"I came to apologize again for the mix-up at the wedding."

Ari's eyebrows rose. "You don't have to do that."

"I'm begging for forgiveness."

"Not necessary."

"The bride and groom are back from their honeymoon—they only took a long weekend—and would like to meet you."

"But Jerry . . ."

"Had confessed all his mistakes to Barbara, who is almost grateful to you for accidentally punishing her husband for his error in judgment." He tested the chowder and winked at Peggy. "Delicious, as always."

"You flatterer, you," she said and continued to chop onions. "It was about time those two settled their differences and quit wasting time. Now they can raise a family, have a life."

"They had a life before they got married," Ari protested dryly.

Peggy shrugged eloquently and stood up. "Come on, Ruthie, let's get some fresh air."

Ruthie seemed content to keep Peggy company. Her mother-in-law's comments and chatter didn't seem to faze her in the least. After they left, Ari said, "That girl is a saint. She works with Mom four days a week and never complains."

"Why should she?"

Ari chose not to answer. Her mother's down-home advice never failed to make her blood pressure rise.

"You're invited to dinner," Max told her.

"Where?"

"At Jerry and Barb's."

"With you."

He nodded. "Naturally."

"Why?"

"I told you—they want to meet you."

"When?"

"Friday." When she didn't say anything he added, "Are you busy that night?"

"No."

"Then say yes."

It was against her better judgment, but she'd told her mother that she could take care of herself and she'd meant it. Believed it. She was one smart lady—smart enough to play with fire and not get burned. Timing and coordination were crucial—and she had an abundance of both. "Yes."

He smiled, and Ari felt her throat go dry. He was a dangerously attractive man. Not model-gorgeous, but the kind of man who looked as if he could take over in an emergency, rescue horses from burning barns, deliver babies on the freeway. A man who didn't mind getting his hands dirty or his feet wet. "I'll pick you up at seven."

"Fine."

"Your folks still live out on Harbor Island?"

"Yes, but not for much longer. They're cleaning out the old place, getting ready to sell it and buy something small."

"What about family dinners?"

"Russ, my oldest brother, is buying the house. He and his wife, Karen, have five kids. They'll inherit the whole Simone clan on holidays."

He ate his soup one spoonful at a time, seeming content to sit in the back of Uncle Harry's market on a Tuesday afternoon. "And how many is that?"

"Russ equals seven. Kevin and Linda have two, so that's eleven. My parents—thirteen. Roscoe and Ruthie are expecting twins in a few months, so that's seventeen. Me, Joe and Jim. Twenty. Linda's parents and two sisters usually are part of any holiday, so that sometimes means twenty-one, minimum." He didn't seem fazed by the numbers. Poor Ruthie had almost gone into shock the first time she'd met all the Simones at a Thanksgiving dinner.

"I have a large family, too." He nodded toward the pile of peeled potatoes as Ari got up to rinse them in the sink. "Now I understand why going to Block Island with me was appealing."

"I had a good time." Ari could feel his gaze on her back and wished she hadn't worn her old jeans and Joey's blue-striped cotton shirt. She wished she didn't smell like raw fish. When she turned back to the table, Max has stood up, tossed his cardboard bowl into the garbage bin, and was reaching into his back pocket for his wallet.

"Don't," she said, looking at the wallet. "This is my treat. I owe you a meal anyway."

"You don't owe me anything."

"Please?"

He put his wallet back and stepped closer. "I'll pick you up at seven o'clock."

"Do you know where I live?"

"No," he lied. Actually he'd looked it up in the phone book and driven by the house twice like a kid with a brand-new driver's license.

Ari gave him directions and Max pretended to pay attention. He wondered if he should press his luck and ask her to the movies tonight. He'd like the darkness, the intimacy of a theater. He would hold her hand and buy her popcorn.

"See you Friday, then," Ari said, giving him a strange look.

"Friday," he echoed as he left the kitchen. No, he'd have to go slowly. This was one lady who wouldn't be rushed.

He'd be patient. That was one of the qualities of a good fisherman—patience, plus optimism and a strong back.

4

"THE PALATINE, a Dutch ship filled with wealthy passengers, blew off course during a storm, ended up on a reef and eventually caught on fire." Jerry paused for breath.

"And?" Ari leaned forward.

"The islanders risked their lives that night to jump in small boats and rescue the people on board. One woman refused to leave her jewels and her gold and went down with the ship."

"What about the others?"

"Safe," Max answered. "But the story changed over the years, making the islanders seem as if they had wrecked the ship, looted it when it was stuck on the reef, then set fire to it. A woman's screams are said to be heard on foggy, stormy nights."

"That story gives me the creeps." Barbara shuddered, her blond curls shaking. She was a tiny woman, with fair skin and an open, friendly manner. Older than Ari would have guessed from her brief inspection during the wedding march, Jerry's wife had greeted Ari warmly. "Sea stories! You two never stop." She rose gracefully from the couch. "I'm going to put dinner on the table before we all starve to death."

Ari set down her wineglass. "Want some help?"

"Sure. I never refuse help in the kitchen—it's not exactly my favorite place." Once in the narrow galley kitchen, Ari watched Barbara open the oven and check the thermometer stuck in a long roll of roast beef. "We don't need gravy, do we?"

"No," Ari said, sensing the other woman didn't want to make it. She didn't want to make it, either.

"Baked potatoes," Barb announced, using a pot holder to grab foil-wrapped lumps from the oven rack. "Nobody can screw up baked potatoes. Not even me." She tossed them into a large bowl, then hauled a bag of corn out of the freezer. "I'll zap this in the microwave, throw the bread in a basket and we're done."

"Perfect," Ari said, feeling more comfortable by the second. "What else can I do to help?"

"Would you get the salad from the refrigerator?"

"Sure" Ari opened the refrigerator while Barbara dumped frozen corn kernels into a glass casserole dish. The salad sat elegantly in an enormous wooden bowl. It was a masterpiece, with cauliflower, spinach leaves, toasted nuts, slices of avocado and tiny curls of bacon. "This is beautiful."

"Oh, thank Jerry. He likes to do salads, while I struggle with everything else."

"I wish you would have let me bring something."

"You brought the wine. That's more than enough."

Ari carefully placed the bowl in the middle of the narrow trestle table in the dining area. White plates rested on woven emerald place mats, and the simple silverware shone as if it were new. Which of course it was. "You've gone to a lot of trouble, Barbara."

"You're our first guests, you know." She chuckled. "We lived together for a few years, but I'm not counting that."

"Counting what?" Jerry asked, entering the room.

"How long we've been together."

"Since your mother paid me to push your stroller," Jerry said, catching Barb's waist. "That was our first date, Mrs. Carter."

"You weren't my only date," she retorted with a laugh. She tossed a mischievous look at Ari. "I always liked older men. I had an awful crush on your brother Roscoe when I was a high school freshman. He was a senior and didn't even know my name."

"He's going to be a father soon," Ari said, thinking of Ruthie's proud awkwardness.

"Lucky man," Max said, joining them. "Twins, right?"

Ari nodded, surprised at his sincerity. "Yes."

Jerry took the chilled wine from the refrigerator. Barbara leaned back against the counter, her arms folded casually in front of her. "I still can't believe we're married."

Jerry gave her a quick kiss before he reached into the drawer for the corkscrew. "Boggles the mind, doesn't it?"

"Especially after the mix-up at the wedding," she continued. "I never even saw Ari, but I couldn't figure out why Max dashed off down the side aisle."

"Neither could I," Ari murmured. "At first I thought he was only trying to be helpful and show me the way out."

"I did," Max said, standing close to her.

"Did you ever get to the wedding you were supposed to go to?"

Obviously Max hadn't told his friends everything. "Uh, no."

Jerry winced. "Sorry. I didn't mean for my mistakes to cause everyone so much trouble."

"Not completely *your* mistake," Max added.

Barbara remained surprisingly cheerful as she patted her husband on the arm. "Cheer up, babe. The past is past. Besides," she said, grabbing the bowl of potatoes, "we may get pregnant and have twins ourselves."

Jerry shuddered, but didn't look too unhappy at the thought as he skillfully eased the cork from the bottle. "Want me to slice the meat?"

"Sure." Barbara put the potatoes onto the table. "You can use the electric knife your cousin gave us as a wedding present."

Max took the wine from Jerry and began to pour the golden liquid into glasses neatly arranged on the table. "Think of the story we'll have to tell our children," he said.

Of course, he meant his own children. Or Jerry's. She kept her voice light. "Uncle Max will be a big hit telling tales like that."

Jerry plugged in the knife. "Uncle Max had better keep his mouth shut!" he shouted over the electric whine.

Max chuckled. "You'd better concentrate on your work, or you'll be minus some fingers when we head out on Sunday."

"Going fishing?" The simple words were deceptive, Ari knew. Commercial fishing was an enormous business, with hundreds of thousand of dollars at stake.

"Yes," Max said. His large hand touched Ari's back through the thin apricot cotton blouse she wore belted over her elegant black pants. Ari moved to break the intriguing contact. She'd resolved to resist Max's seductive charm, but it wasn't easy. Ari turned to smile at him, pleased with herself for being able to control her skin's reaction.

"These two won't quit," Barb told her. "They've plenty ashore to keep them busy, but they still head out to sea every chance they get."

"Why?"

"It's in our blood," Max teased.

Ari knew she should have known the answer to that one. She'd heard it all her life.

"After this trip, we'll take turns, all right?"

Barbara nodded. "I'll believe it when I see it." She motioned to Ari. "Let's eat." She followed Jerry to the table. He set down the platter of meat as Max and Ari took the seats across from each other. Barbara picked up her wineglass. "I have a toast," she said.

"Isn't the man of the house supposed to do that?" Jerry grumbled.

She shook her head, much to Ari's amusement. "This is the nineties, babe." She smiled at Max and Ari and lifted her glass high. "To friendship, love and . . ."

"And?" Jerry prompted, looking longingly at the roast beef.

"And . . . fidelity."

"I think there's a message in there somewhere," Max observed.

"Yeah. And I got the hint." Jerry clicked his glass against his wife's.

Max touched Ari's glass with his own. "To love, Arianna." he said.

"To friendship," she countered.

"To fish!" Jerry added, breaking the spell. "To a few hundred thousand pounds of scup."

The women nodded, knowing that these days nets full of the bronze-colored fish meant a profitable trip.

Max paused before taking a swallow of wine. "I won't argue with that."

Ari grinned at him. "That's a first," she commented. "I thought you liked to argue about everything."

Jerry reached for Ari's salad bowl and shot an amused look at his friend. "Looks like she has you all figured out, Cole."

"COME ON," Max prompted. "How long has it been since you've walked on the beach?"

"Yesterday," Ari fibbed.

"I don't believe you." He opened the car door and climbed out. The salt air came in thick and strong, waves crashed with a soft roar a few yards away. "Let's walk," he said.

Ari reluctantly stepped out of the car and stood on the worn pavement of the parking area at the Narragansett Town Beach. Wide, clean and easily accessible, it was one of the most beautiful beaches in Rhode Island. A hop over the concrete wall that curved between the beach and the sidewalk meant she'd feel the fine sand between her toes and the unfamiliar pull on her thighs that only walking in the sand could bring.

Dark figures sat on the wall. It was a gathering place, and had been long before urban renewal had changed the rambunctious beach town of the fifties and sixties into a tidy tourist attraction. Now tri-story town houses faced the ocean. Their rear side curved around another parking area; the ground floors held stores where one could buy ice cream, souvenirs, jewelry or doughnuts. Opposite were a bank, movie theater and grocery store. A large hotel and a gourmet Spanish restaurant completed the resort. All of the buildings were new, shingled, with pale weathered wood with white trim or the forest green so popular in the Victorian era, when large cottages—summer homes of the wealthy—had lined the Pier Village sidewalks.

But now night beckoned, and Max waited with an outstretched hand to walk in the pale shaft of moonlight that highlighted the sand. It was a little too romantic, Ari decided. For some reason Max and she ended up in the strangest places. "It's awfully quiet."

He took her hand as if it were the most natural thing to do. "That's what I had in mind."

She felt the familiar clasp of his fingers and wondered why she felt secure. Why she felt happy. "I think we've been through this before."

"Don't worry. There isn't a boat in sight." He tugged her through the opening in the chain-link fence near the end of the seawall. "Come on. You grew up here. Didn't any of your boyfriends take you walking along the beach at night?"

"No," she fibbed again, her voice threatening to crack. The question hit a little too close to home, and she pushed the memories deep inside where they belonged—safe, tucked away, not to be brought out to be examined even by the dim light of the moon.

Max didn't argue. His fingers tightened around hers, as if he sensed something was wrong. She stopped to slip off her sandals and held on to the straps with one finger. The sand was cold between her toes, a pleasant counterpoint to the warm, humid air. June in Rhode Island could be hot or rainy, she remembered. Humid, too—an unpleasant weather condition Westerners luckily couldn't even comprehend.

They walked silently along the shore, Ari careful not to step into the path of the water that was scraping rhythmically along the sand.

"How are you going to spend the rest of your summer?" he asked finally.

"What do you mean?"

"Working? Going to the beach?"

"I might get a job," she said, "if I think I'll go crazy peeling potatoes every day with Mom and Ruth. There's a lot to do in the house, too."

"When are your parents moving?"

"As soon as we get the house packed up, cleaned out and all that. By September, though. Mom doesn't seem to be in any hurry, and that's why I came home for the summer. She conned me into thinking she needed me, but now I'm beginning to get suspicious."

"And restless."

"Yes," she said, surprised that he'd noticed. "I may look for a job scooping ice cream."

"A college professor making ice-cream cones—now that I'd have to see."

"It would be a good change," she argued. "I want to do something totally unrelated to books, papers, grades and lectures." The warm breeze whipped her hair across her face, but she didn't drop Max's hand to brush it away.

"The door is always open at Cole Products."

"I'm not very good at packing fish."

"I was thinking more along the line of office work. I'm always desperate for help, especially when I'm out to sea."

"How can you manage a business like that and still go out?"

"I can't," he said. "But it's hard to give it up for a desk job."

Give up what? she wanted to ask. *A life-risking occupation alone at sea?* "Time to turn back," she said instead. "We've gone far enough."

"A symbolic statement?"

She shrugged. "I guess you could interpret it that way."

He stopped, turning to face her, and gently tugged her against his hard body until the tips of her breasts touched his cotton shirt.

"Max—"

"Shh," he said, his lips curving slightly. "I don't want to hear what you're going to say."

"Rude man," she returned softly, without anger, as he looped his arms around her waist. All protests remained unspoken when she looked into his shadowed eyes. *You might as well kiss the man and get it over with. Get it out of your system, once and for all.*

"Now you're insulting me again," Max murmured, bending lower to brush her mouth with his lips. She trembled, a totally involuntary reaction—and perfectly normal, she told herself, on a breezy June night by the sea. "You'll hurt my feelings," he teased, lifting his head slightly to look into her eyes.

"I doubt it." The brief kiss had left her unsatisfied, wanting what he'd held back. She'd barely felt his lips before he lifted his head. *Not fair, Captain, but probably wise.*

"No," he argued, brushing his lips back and forth against hers, easing, waiting. "You've crushed me. I'll never be the same."

Oh, hell. Ari dropped her sandals and put her hands upon his broad shoulders. She could feel the strength there, the power of a man who worked outdoors, a man who worked hard. His lips continued to tease hers, a tantalizing touch of warmth that threatened to dissolve every muscle in her body. Her fingers sought the smooth skin of his neck and tangled in his hair, the kiss deepened and his tongue searched and parted her lips.

Ari couldn't breathe. She didn't want to. Her heart pounded and she melted. She was too close to the fire. Ready to be burned up in the glow of a reckless decision. Her toes curled into the wind-chilled sand, and she stood on tiptoe to cling to Max as they kissed.

A cold little wave tickled her ankles and made her jump. Max released her mouth and they both struggled for breath. He stroked her hair. She rested her head first up on his chest, then in the hollow beneath his shoulder, and waited for her heart to return to its normal pattern.

"I told you on the island that we were meant for each other," he murmured, but there was a gentle, teasing affection in his voice, so Ari didn't know how serious he was.

"No, you didn't." She would have remembered a statement like that, teasing or otherwise.

"I thought it, then. Maybe I was too afraid to say it out loud."

She was glad her face was tucked into his chest so he couldn't see how embarrassed she was. "You're not afraid of anything."

There was silence as he continued to stroke her hair. "I'm afraid you won't see me again." When she was silent, he added, "I'm afraid you won't give us a chance."

"There's no us, Max." She didn't know how she could say something so untrue after a heart-stopping kiss like the one they'd shared, but gave it her best shot.

"There could be."

The man didn't give up. "Only for the summer." She looked up at him. "That's all I can give."

"That's not all I want."

At least he was honest. She had to give him credit for that. She stepped out of his arms, picked up her sandals and turned back the way they'd come. But there was no reason to drag this out. No reason at all to encourage what could only be a temporary affair—although it had the potential of being one of those incredible memories that made old women smile. And she didn't need the complicating factor of passion to interfere in an already full summer. Full of relatives. Full of advice, of uncomfortable reminders of the life she could have had and now wanted no part of. "I need to go home."

Max nodded and took her hand once again until they reached the wall. Later, when he parked the car in front of the large Simone house, Max broke the silence. "Perhaps we should go to Block Island again."

"You're going out to sea Sunday," she said, more as a reminder to herself than to him. His profile was a strong line in the shadowed car, his eyes dark as he watched her.

"I'll be back."

"Well, good luck." She reached for the handle on her side before he could operate his. "Stay where you are," she said. "You don't have to walk me to the door."

He frowned. She knew that irritated the hell out of him, so hopped quickly out of the car to stand in the darkness. Now he wouldn't be able to argue. Max opened his door, got out and stood up, looking at her over the roof of the car. "You're a difficult woman, Ari Simone."

. "I like it that way," she told him, turned and walked into the pool of light from the front door. She could feel his gaze on her back, so she didn't look back at him before she pulled the front door open and went inside into the stuffy warmth of the dark living room. *It's better this way,* she told herself, tiptoeing up the stairs to her room. Better to stay away from charming sea captains, no matter what century she lived in.

"WHY DO YOU WANT to go out and get a job?" Peggy Simone put her hands upon her ample hips and shook her head. "You've got a job right here."

Ari paid no attention to her mother's question, having heard it four times already this Friday and approximately seventy times during the past week. She continued to sort through the stack of newspapers piled on the counter. Peggy saved newspapers the way other people collected souvenirs.

"Don't look at that trash—the boys keep bringing it home."

Ari lifted a thick copy of *Single Connection* from the stack. "What is this?"

"Ads," Ruthie explained, "for dates. I think it comes out every week."

Intrigued, Ari unfolded the paper and started reading. "Maybe I'll find a nice farmer in here," she said, trying to tease her mother.

"You've got a nice fisherman," Peggy muttered.

Ari looked up and grinned at Ruthie. "Here's one." She bent over the paper and began to read. "Attractive, young, lively, early thirties single male."

"Sounds good so far."

Ari continued. "Desires—"

"*Desires?*"

Ari nodded at her sister-in-law. "Gets right to the point, doesn't he? *Desires* bright, attractive, slim, well-adjusted lady, nonsmoker, no drugs, who likes dining out, traveling, bowling and outdoor pursuits." She looked at her mother. "So what do you think? Is he Mr. Right?"

Peggy shook her head. "You can do better."

"Okay." Ari continued to read. "You know, this isn't a bad idea. Some of these men sound wonderful."

"Not just men advertise," Ruthie observed.

"Here's a man who needs help raising his children." Ari turned the page and resumed reading. "Here's an ad that's four inches long—the guy tells everything about himself at once. Says he's independently wealthy."

Peggy sniffed. "You can't believe everything you read."

"Have Joey and Jimmy ever answered these ads?"

Ruth shook her head. "I doubt it. They're too young, I think. They meet too many girls in the bars as it is."

Ari read through the entire paper, much to Peggy's disgust and Ruthie's entertainment. Some of the ads were a little strange, but most seemed to be sincere attempts to meet someone with similar interests.

"Good thing it's a slow day," Peggy complained.

The younger women ignored her. Ari went on reading. "I've seen these ads in Personal columns before, but I've never seen a whole paper devoted to them."

"I'm glad I found my husband the old-fashioned way," Ruthie said with a sigh. "I think it's easier than writing an advertisement."

"But it's practical," Ari insisted. "Especially if a person is too busy with work to meet other people or doesn't want to go to bars or has certain preferences—" She stopped, an outrageous thought flashing through her head. No, she couldn't answer any of these ads on Max's behalf. That wouldn't be fair. But—

"What?" Ruth asked.

Ari shook her head. "Nothing. I was just thinking this could be the answer to my problems."

Peggy turned from the stove to frown at her daughter. "Hah!"

Ari folded the paper and tucked it into her bag. "You never know," she said. *If Max placed his own ad he'd be swamped with women and would leave me alone.* She wiped the large counter with a soapy cloth, adding a pine scent to the clam odors that permeated the kitchen. She finished the job and dried her hands on a paper towel before looking at her mother again. "I've got to find something else to do. I think peeling potatoes is driving me crazy," she muttered.

"It's the captain, isn't it?" Peggy shook a finger at her daughter. "The *Million* was due in port yesterday, but your father heard they ran into good fish and are fillin' the holds now."

"Is that so?"

"Don't pretend you're not interested."

"I'm not pretending anything, Mom. I just don't think I can spend the rest of the summer peeling potatoes."

"Rest of the summer? You've only been here a few weeks."

"And you haven't started cleaning out the house yet, either."

Peggy sniffed. "I haven't had time."

"I have, but you've been avoiding it like the plague."

"I'm a busy woman with a business to run."

"Fine," Ari said. "I'll borrow a ladder from Russell and start on the attic." Ari knew the temperature would be about 110°, but she wasn't going to complain. The sooner she helped with the house, the sooner she could go home to Bozeman. It was only July 6; August wasn't too late to make a trip to the Tetons and do a little hiking.

An hour later she surveyed the stuffy, dusty attic and knew why her mother had been avoiding the place. A lifetime's accumulation of possessions filled the large top story of the house. A tribe of Simones working half the day could make a dent in it, but that was what it would take. Ari vowed to organize the project. Every one of the brothers would be required to help clean. Ari slowly backed down the steps.

"It's good to see you again," a low voice murmured.

Ari started and looked down to where Max stood, hands in his pockets, surveying her behind in the dusty shorts. "You could have made me fall off the ladder," she complained.

"I would've caught you."

He held out his hands as if to prove it, and Ari smiled but ignored the urge to tumble into his embrace. Instead she kept a firm grip on the rungs of the ladder and finished stepping down the remaining feet to the floor.

"I thought you were still out."

"We came in this morning, only a few hours ago."

"Why are you here?" She knew there would be much for him to do at the dock.

"I couldn't wait to see you," he said, his blue eyes twinkling. Once again Ari couldn't tell if his words were teasing or serious.

"You cleaned up first."

"Of course."

He looked tired. She guessed he'd had little sleep and knew he would have worked round the clock to bring in a good haul to pay for the expensive new boat he and Jerry were so proud of. "How was the trip?"

Max smiled, looking as pleased as a cat who'd just made a successful dinner of the family's goldfish. "It was a good one," he said, putting his large hands on her shoulders. "And I need someone to celebrate with."

She shook her head. "Don't you have a girlfriend?"

"She's very difficult. Keeps telling me she only likes cowboys."

"She does."

"I told you I wanted a chance to change your mind." He brushed his lips softly against hers.

"No," she said, enjoying the kiss. Once he lifted his head she said, "You can't."

"Can't what?"

"Change her mind."

"I'm a very determined man."

Ari attempted to step back, but his arms tightened around her. "It won't do you any good."

"Have dinner with me tonight and tell me all about it."

She laughed. "Max, you and I are going to be friends."

"I don't need another friend," he growled.

"I'll have dinner with you," she said, knowing she shouldn't, but unable to resist the lure of his eyes. He was fun to be with, he made her laugh, and if she could stop him from kissing her she'd be in pretty good shape. "But you have to stop kissing me all the time."

"Why? It's very enjoyable."

"Because we're going to be friends," she stated simply. Any other relationship with a fisherman was out of the question.

"I don't want any more friends," he repeated. "I want you."

"You can't have me," she said cheerfully, pulling him downstairs and through the hall into the kitchen. "I'm going back home in a few weeks."

"I could change your mind," he said again.

"No." Ari turned to face him, her brown eyes suddenly serious. Her voice was gentle as she looked up at the handsome man who faced her. "You can't, Max. I don't want to stay here. I don't want to spend the rest of my life in Galilee waiting for the boats to come in."

He frowned. "There's more to this than just mountains, isn't there?"

Ari nodded. "Look," she said, "I'm not the right woman for you."

"Have dinner with me anyway. We'll talk about it."

We'll do more than talk about it, Ari decided, thinking of the newspaper tucked in her purse. "Give me some time to get ready?"

"Is an hour and a half enough time?"

She nodded and Max left. He knew Ari was wrong. He climbed into his truck and headed into the Pier to return his library books and select new ones. Then he went out to the IGA to stock up on groceries, since he'd be going back out on the *Million* the day after tomorrow. From the pile of paperwork he'd seen waiting for him on his desk at the plant, he needed to stay home and take care of business on land soon. With Arianna around, that might not be such a hardship, after all.

He had a good crew and a growing business as a sea-food packing plant, but there was a lot of money at stake and the boat mortgage to pay off.

Arianna was exactly the right woman for him. He grew hard just thinking about her softness, her brown eyes, and the way her lips moved under his mouth. She was under his skin, and all of the hours of prowling the deck of the *Million* hadn't given him time to decide how to convince her. Only that he had to.

5

"I HAVE the perfect solution." Ari leaned closer to Max, ignoring with difficulty the romantic nature of the darkened ocean-side restaurant. The flame flickered on the low candle centered between them on the tiny round table.

Max leaned forward. "Solution to what?"

"Our problem."

Max smiled. "Let me guess. You're coming home with me tonight and won't leave for at least fifty years."

"Be serious."

"I am serious," Max said calmly, resting his wineglass on the ivory tablecloth before meeting Ari's impatient expression.

She hesitated. She really didn't believe him for a minute, but the man was definitely persistent. "You have trouble meeting women, don't you?"

He looked insulted, making Ari want to laugh. "I admit that the episode in the church was a little extreme, but it wasn't because I lack for dates. Until now I haven't met anyone special."

"I'm going to help. I have it all figured out." Ari waited while the waitress removed their empty plates and left the dessert menu.

"Interesting," Max said. "How you could figure it all out in just a few hours."

"I got the idea from the newspaper." She ignored the sarcasm and, with satisfaction in her voice, announced, "The personal ads."

Max looked horrified, as if she'd suggested auctioning himself off on the village green. "Oh, no."

"It's perfect." *And the less temptation around me, the better.*

His voice grew louder. "No."

"Why not? You could specify exactly what kind of woman you were interested in."

"Sounds too much like ordering from the Sears catalog."

"You have a better idea?"

"Yes. Forget this and come away with me."

Ari pulled a small notebook from her purse and dug out a pen. "Single white male," she recited. "Wants permanent—you do want a permanent relationship, don't you?"

"Oh, by all means." She ignored the sarcasm.

"Single white male wants permanent—no, better make that lasting relationship with right woman." Max glared at her, and she paused to ask, "Specifications?"

"What?"

"Height, weight, age, interests in common?"

"How old are you?"

"Thirty-two, but—"

"Fine. Thirty-two, then." He nodded toward the pad. "You'd better start writing this down."

She picked up the pen and did as he said. "And?"

"I usually go for tall Amazon-style blondes...."

Ari squashed a surprising pang of jealousy. "Is that all?"

"I'm thinking." She waited, wishing Max didn't look like a man who was in the throes of a passionate reminiscence. "Redheads, too," he added finally.

"Anything else, like a special interest?" She waited impatiently in the silence, and the waitress came over to ask if they'd like to order dessert.

"Ari?"

"Cheesecake and coffee, please."

Max nodded to the waitress. "Make that two."

Ari tapped her pen against the paper. "Anything else?"

"I'm not going into detail about my . . . special interests with you, Ari."

"What about children? A lot of women are single parents now, you know."

"Children are okay."

"Likes children," she wrote. "What about a non-smoker?"

He shrugged. "I don't care. I respect other people's vices."

"Tolerant. Is that it?"

"You tell me."

She reviewed her notes. "That should do it."

"Where is this thing going—you're not really serious, are you?"

Ari smiled at him and nodded. "Very serious, Captain. But the ad will be confidential, will go to a post office box at the paper with a code number, which I'll be responsible for."

"This isn't going in the Providence *Journal*, is it?"

"No, there's a paper specifically for this kind of thing—a very respectable paper, no kinky sex ads or anything like that," she said. "It also has all sorts of classes you can take to meet people. Not sleazy at all.

I need to get this in by noon tomorrow so it will be in Tuesday's edition."

"So I'm just expanding my horizons?" he inquired.

"Exactly."

The cheesecake arrived and Max picked up his fork, still uncertain. "Add passionate somewhere in that ad, will you, Ari?"

Ari felt an unexpected pain in her heart at the thought of Max being passionate with a strange woman—a tall, blond, athletic woman—but quickly banished the thought and refused to allow herself to be jealous of the person who would share the rest of Max's summer. The idea was to get him occupied with someone else so she would be free to clean out the attic, make chowder and get out of Rhode Island as quickly as possible. She didn't need a handsome, sexy sea captain screwing up her plans. Sea captains were definitely not on her list of eligible men.

Max pushed his plate away. "It's not going to work, you know."

"Why not?"

"I want you. Nobody else."

The intensity of his tone took her breath away. No one had ever said quite those words to her. There was something so compelling and appealing about his directness. Those blue eyes challenged her, and Ari struggled to keep her voice light. "You don't even know me."

"We have years to work on knowing each other."

"Max . . ."

"Forget it," he said, reaching for his coffee. "It's going to be a long summer."

Arianna could agree with that. Being in Rhode Island certainly made it appear that way. She shoved the notebook at him. "Come on. Give it a chance."

He stared at her for a long moment. "That's what I've been asking of you."

Ari felt heat rise into her face, but her eyes never wavered from his gaze. "So what do you say?"

"I don't think you can find a woman in this entire state I'd rather be with than you. But go ahead and try. It's a waste of time."

"You need to date more."

"My feelings exactly."

"Then?"

"All right," he agreed, looking away from her. "You can place the ad. That doesn't mean I'll do anything with the responses. That is, if there are any."

"Fair enough." Ari felt a little suspicious of his new attitude. Was he up to something?

"I already have a box at the Narragansett post office." He gave her the number. "You pay for the ad."

Ari nodded, picking up her fork. "It will be worth it."

"Maybe," Max said. "Guess we'll just have to wait and see, won't we?"

SHE HAD TO WAIT for a foggy day, a Monday, when the boats swayed uselessly in dock and the boys were home, roaming the house and eating anything they could find in the refrigerator. Her father, alternating between contentment with his retired state and frustration because he felt the boys didn't know what they were doing, roamed behind them, asking questions that began with, "Did you make sure that—?"

"It's time," Ari announced, but no one paid any attention to her. Jim and Joe argued over who would get to read the sports section and which movie they would go see this afternoon.

"We're going to go up and clean out the attic."

Incredulous looks.

"We've got to get ready for the yard sale." Ari pointed to the stairs. "I put an ad in *The Narragansett Times*, so there's no backing out. And I borrowed a ladder. With the four of us, we should be able to at least get a start on it. Otherwise I'll throw out everything that belongs to you, including the twelve years of *Playboy* magazines stacked in the east corner."

Rusty Simone eyed his sons with satisfaction. Here at least was a job he could supervise and have some control over. "Boys, we have work to do."

They knew better than to argue. Hours later Ari was dirty, tired, and sneezing from the dust. Russell brought his pickup truck to the back door, the crew carried trash and made trips to the dump. Ari examined anything that had sentimental value and put it in the living room for her mother to check. Anything worth saving for the yard sale went into the garage, to be priced another time. The boys worked until they begged for mercy. Someone promised someone else a cold beer if the job could be finished by five o'clock.

But Ari had no mercy. She'd come home to do a job this summer and wouldn't rest until it was done.

Peggy was in Galilee, not due back until suppertime. When they heard her voice at the door, four of her six children sighed with relief.

"Oh, my God!" Peggy cried, still panting. "I've never seen such a mess in my life!"

"The boxes are labeled according to whose stuff is inside," Ari explained. "The rest of it is waiting for a turn in the truck to the dump."

"My goodness!" Peggy exclaimed. "There's so much of it."

"You wouldn't believe what we threw out."

Peggy sat down. "I suppose not." She surveyed her daughter, who was covered in dust and looked like Raggedy Ann on a bad day. "You'd better get cleaned up."

Ari shook her head. "Not until we've finished here. I want to get this stuff to the dump. If I had a sticker on the car I'd make a few trips myself."

"I really think you should clean up."

"Why?"

"Your captain is home. He stopped in a while ago and I told him you'd be home tonight."

"Oh, Mom." Why couldn't her mother stay out of her business? "I wish you hadn't."

"I thought you were . . . friends."

"We are. That's all. Friends."

"Well—" her mother sniffed "—how am I supposed to ignore a man who obviously wants to see more of my daughter? Am I so unfeeling as to turn him away when he shows up at the store and asks for you?"

"Yes." Ari stifled a pang of guilt. She wondered if Max had checked his mailbox. She'd placed the ad in last week's edition of *Single Connection* and hadn't warned him that his post office box would soon be stuffed with responses from unknown women. She hadn't seen Max in ten days. Ten very long days.

"Well, I didn't." Peggy pointed to the stairs. "You go get cleaned up and I'll have the boys finish this. You did a good job, Arianna, and I'm pleased that we've made a start. Thinking of cleaning this place gave me nightmares."

Ari patted her mother's shoulder. "Don't worry. That's why you had six kids—we have to help you out sometimes, you know."

"I suppose. You could help me by being nice to Max."

"I'm always nice to Max." Ari thought of the kisses they'd shared. Nice was too mild a word for the feeling that she'd had to deal with on a physical level.

"He's a good man, Ari."

"I know, Mom," Ari said. "But I'm going back home soon, and I can't get involved with Max, no matter what kind of person he is."

Peggy sighed. "Have it your way, love, but you've been running away from Rhode Island since Eddie died. Staying away from here isn't going to make the past go away."

"It makes it bearable," Ari muttered. "And that's all I need."

Peggy shook her head. "You and Eddie were close, very close, and I know you loved him very much."

Ari nodded, her throat closing so she couldn't speak.

"But it's time you were over it, time you went on. Eight years is a long time to be alone."

"I haven't been alone."

"No?" Peggy cocked an eyebrow.

"No," her daughter said firmly.

Peggy's voice grew softer. "You're thirty-two, no husband, no lover, no children."

"Thank you for the kind reminder."

Peggy winced. "I didn't mean to hurt your feelings— I just want to see you happy."

"And I have to be left alone to decide for myself what makes me happy." With that, Ari left the room and headed back upstairs. Instead of loading another batch of trash onto Kevin's truck, she went into her bedroom, where Joey had shoved three cardboard boxes with her name scrawled across one side. She pushed them against the patterned wall and sat down on the bed, trying to remember she was thirty-two and not thirteen. She felt like thirteen, though, and hated the feeling. How could her family have the power to reduce her from a capable English professor to an incompetent, lonely child in a matter of seconds?

The knock on the door surprised her. "Come in."

Peggy slowly opened the door. "I came to apologize. I had no right."

Ari's heart was suddenly full.

"It's just that we miss you."

Peggy closed the door and Ari sighed, feeling better, guessing it was better to be loved too much than not at all. Even so, there were some days when being the middle child in such a large, overwhelming family felt like more than she could handle and still stay sane.

IN LESS THAN AN HOUR Max stood at the door to the Simone house, waiting for someone to answer his knock. Ari was damn well going to get him out of the mess she'd gotten him into. His aggravation, however, faded when she opened the door and smiled up at him, her dark eyes twinkling with good humor. She looked and smelled wonderful, as if she'd just stepped out of the shower. She wore some kind of pink dress that skimmed her body to her knees. Max fought off his caveman instincts and carefully kept his expression neutral.

"Hi, Captain."

"Hi, yourself," he said, allowing a brief smile to crease his face.

She stepped back to let him in, but he stood his ground. "I'm not here for a visit, Ari. I got into port last night, and I just came from the post office."

He didn't have to spell it out for her. "How many?"

"A very large pile. Too many to count."

Ari looked pleased that her scheme was working so well. "Where are they?"

"In the car. I haven't opened them yet."

"Oh, good. Were you waiting for me?"

"I was trying to decide if I should throw them in the garbage and forget this whole crazy idea of yours."

"But you didn't."

Max sighed. "Then I came to my senses and wondered what on earth I would do with myself when you went back to Indiana."

"Montana," she corrected.

"Whatever," he conceded with a shrug. "I could get pretty lonely."

"You're going to be real lonely in about ten seconds if you don't quit teasing me."

"You want to see the letters?"

"You have to ask?"

"It's probably pretty private stuff. You might get jealous."

"I'll try to control myself. Come on, let's see if we can find you some likely candidates."

He frowned. "This isn't such a good idea, Ari."

She followed him out to the car and saw the pile of mail on the leather seat. "Wow, you're a really hot item!"

"I don't want to do this."

"You might find someone interesting, you know. After all, you dared me to try to find someone for you, remember?"

"I must have been out of my mind at the time from too many lonely days at sea."

She picked one up and sniffed. A potent perfume scented the envelope. "Nice. Let's start with this one."

"Not here," he grumbled. "I'm not going to sit in this hot car, and I'm not going into the house to have your family join in the hunt."

"Then where?"

"Aboard the *Million*."

"Now?"

He shook his head. "The Blessing of the Fleet is this weekend."

Ari remembered. The holiday for boaters and fishermen had gained wide popularity among tourists in the last twenty years. What had started out as a simple ceremony to protect fishermen by blessing their boats had become a tourist weekend, with open houses and parties on boats, a parade through the Harbor of Refuge and even a road race for those who liked to jog through the streets of Narragansett for ten miles. "I know."

"Come to the *Million*. Spend the day with me."

"You're turning down a day of fishing?"

He shrugged. "She needs a couple of parts and they're being shipped. And I—I have work to do at the plant."

"I'm not comfortable on the ocean," she said, hoping he'd change his mind.

"Then I'll dump the letters overboard."

"You're impossible," she said with a laugh, but knew that she did want to see the letters. She'd begun to care about this man. All the same, there was no way she was going to let herself fall in love, even if Max was a special, wonderful person who deserved more than

empty nights at the Neptune with his fishing buddies.
He didn't need her, any more than she needed him.

"Come, my love, what do you say?"

"I'm not your love."

"Figure of speech."

Ari considered her options. She would have to be involved in the upcoming weekend one way or another.
Being with Max was definitely the way she'd preferred
to spend the day. Her family was getting on her nerves
more than usual.

"All right," she said. "It's a deal."

"I NEVER SAID I'd go out with any of them."

The late-afternoon sun was hot on Ari's shoulders as
she sat on the deck of the *Million* and surveyed the man
leaning on the railing. She'd carefully separated the
piles of letters into Never in a Million years, Possibili-
ties and Definitely Worth Pursuing. She picked up the
pile of Worth Pursuing and shook them at Max. "What
do you think these are, then? A seventh-grade writing
exercise? These women are interested in meeting you."

"I'm not interested in meeting them."

Ari sighed, tucked the pile beside her and absently
adjusted the top of her bathing suit so that the tops of
her breasts weren't too exposed. One sunny-yellow
strap kept falling off her shoulder and she finally gave
up and left it there.

"You're going to get burned if you're not careful."

"I'm careful," she said.

"Did you have fun?"

"Yes." She smiled at Max, her attention centered on
him for a brief moment. "It was a wonderful day." To
her surprise, it really had been. She'd met old friends
and made new ones, and Barbara and she had taken

turns with the chores involved when entertaining on a fishing boat. An interesting day, and one she'd share with her friends at the university when she returned. What I Did on My Summer Vacation. "Thanks for not going out of the bay."

"We could have gone with the rest of them to Block Island."

Ari looked out toward the island and the large expanse of sea between Point Judith and New Harbor. "No, thanks. I like being tied up to the dock."

"It smells."

She sniffed. "I guess I never notice it."

"Good thing," he said, coming to sit beside her. Oh, he was handsome all right, with his worn jeans and clean T-shirt the color of a summer morning sky. "Want a turkey sandwich?"

Ari shook her head. "Didn't you eat today?"

"No time."

"You were too busy talking."

"I like that."

"Talk to me?" she asked, knowing she was treading on dangerous ground, but her sunglasses kept her eyes hidden, so she could be a little braver.

"Not about these women." He pushed the pile away so he was closer to Ari, his knees almost touching hers.

"Don't," she warned, grabbing the papers. "They'll blow away."

"Fine."

"We had a deal."

"Right. I let you open them if you came today."

"That's not the only deal, Max."

He tugged her sunglasses off her ears and dropped them onto the deck. "I'm not going to find a woman I want as much as you, Ari, no matter how many envelopes you open and how many piles you make or how many ads you put in the classifieds." His lips were too close to hers, but Ari didn't move. She just watched those beautiful lips move as he continued. "I want you, Arianna Simone, and you have to realize that."

She touched his face in a tentative gesture—she didn't know if it was to make him stop talking or to bring him closer. She remembered the warmth of that mouth against hers, and the answering heat of his body on the beach that night. All of a sudden it seemed like a long time ago.

Too long.

He touched her lips with his, a brief-touching kiss that was over before she could respond. He did it again, three times, until her fingers splayed against his jaw in silent demand. Asking for trouble. Not caring if she found it.

She found it, all right, because he took her mouth with his tongue then, seeking her warmth and her taste, pulling her closer when he felt her answering motions. He held her to him and they tumbled onto the hard deck of the *Million* in the twilight, as the sun's rays faded over the bay. Ari barely felt the wood beneath her or the coil of rope that scraped her elbow as she lifted her hand to the side of Max's neck.

The kiss continued, an electrifying caress of lips and tongues. It was as if they belonged together, as if it should continue for the rest of their lives.

An unnerving thought. Ari struggled for some self-control, but could feel herself sinking into the fathomless trap of passion. She tried desperately to ignore what her body was telling her—that she wanted this man and wanted him now.

Now wasn't a good time. This man wasn't the right one.

He lifted his head as if he could sense her withdrawal. His blue eyes gazed down at her; he looked happy. "See?"

"See what?"

He hesitated, and Ari had the impression he wouldn't say what he'd been going to. "I told you you'd have a good time today."

"Mmm." She smoothed his hair and sighed. "I think you should get off of me now."

"Uh-uh. This is the best part of the day—lying on top of you on board a rocking boat." He grinned wickedly. "We hardly have to move."

"I don't feel any rocking," she protested, but didn't push him away. She allowed herself a few more moments with the luxury of Max's body pressed against her own.

"Mmm," he murmured in turn, tasting her neck with tiny kisses. "Maybe it was just wishful thinking."

"What if people saw us?"

"I'd tell them you fell and I was checking your body for bruises." He raised his head and propped himself up on one elbow, leaving his other hand free to skim the remaining bathing suit strap off Ari's shoulder. "No marks there, he drawled.

"Touch anything but my shoulder and you're a dead man."

His warm, rough hand paused above the smooth swell of breast. One finger outlined the suit's bodice. "I'd chance it."

Ari decided it was time to put a stop to lovely sexual meanderings on a hot, sultry summer evening. Making love to Max would be as easy as spreading suntan lotion, but she knew she'd be taking on more than a one-nighter with a handsome stranger.

"Sorry, Captain." She cleared her throat and hoped she sounded casual as she attempted to wriggle herself free.

Max rolled off her and lay on his back, looking up into the twilight sky. "Hungry?"

Suddenly she was. "Uh-huh. Are you?"

"Yeah."

"What kind of food?"

He thought for a minute. "Italian."

"Okay." Ari sat up and briefly bent to kiss him on the cheek. "Friends?"

"Not quite," he growled, watching her fold the Worth Pursuing pile of letters into a neat packet. "What are you going to do with them?"

"I'm going to put them into the glove compartment of your truck for safekeeping."

"Come on, then. Let's drive over to Terminesi's. If you won't make love with me, the least you can do is buy me a meatball sandwich."

She would have bought him anything. But first she wanted to change out of her bathing suit, so he drove her to her house and waited for her while she changed into a sundress. When she came downstairs her parents beamed.

"What a nice couple, Rusty, don't you think?" Peggy looked as if she could explode with happiness.

"Ayeh." Her father nodded, his red beard going up and down, up and down, doing his Yankee fisherman imitation. It used to make her laugh when she was a little girl. It didn't get a smile now.

Ari blew them a kiss and grabbed Max's arm as she headed for the door. "Well, I'm happy that you're happy."

"They're driving me crazy," she muttered once they were safely outside.

"What about me?" Max asked when they were out the door and heading across the tiny scrap of lawn that faced the road.

Ari glanced up at him, wondering if he was teasing again. She assumed he was. "You're driving me crazy, too."

"Good," he said, settling her into the car. "It ought to be mutual."

HE TREATED HER like a big brother for the rest of the evening, teasing her gently from time to time, introducing her to people she vaguely remembered from years ago who looked curiously at the two of them sitting together in the popular restaurant. When Roscoe and Ruthie walked into the crowded restaurant, Max waved.

"What are you doing?" Ari asked.

"Seeing if they want to join us," Max said.

They did, and the waitress let them slide over to a larger table. Soon Joey and Jimmy stepped in for a pizza and to see who was there. The boys accepted Max's welcoming handshake and pulled extra chairs up to the table.

"Why don't you call my parents and see if they want to come down, too?"

Max shrugged. "Touchy, aren't you?"

Ari laughed, but inside she felt steamrolled. She was now surrounded by her family, everyone joking back and forth. It should have been an intrusion, but in fact it was fun. Ruthie, usually quiet, told a funny story about the chowder and one of Peggy's unsatisfied customers, and had them in tears laughing. Jimmy and Joey conned Max into buying a pizza, and when Russ and Karen entered the restaurant, Ari gave up.

Max and Russ exchanged a few sea stories and Karen, always sociable, greeted friends throughout the restaurant before joining Russ at the table across from Ari. She waved, unable to have a conversation over the other, exuberant Simone voices. Karen laughed and ordered a diet soda and a couple of platters of veal parmigiana from the waitress.

"We're missing Kevin," Ari said.

"The baby-sitter got sick," Ruthie supplied. "If they could find someone else they were going to meet us at the nine o'clock show."

"Which one?"

"The new one with Mel Gibson."

Ari felt Max's fingers lightly touch the nape of her neck, gently requesting her attention. She turned to him, her thigh pleasantly scrunched against his in the now-crowded booth.

"Want to go to the movies?" His hand caressed her shoulder, bringing unwanted visions of sitting together in a dark theater for a couple of hours. It sounded more appetizing than she was willing to admit.

"I really like M-Mel Gibson," she stammered.

"So do I."

He nodded toward Karen. "Mind if we join you?"

"Course not," she said. "The more the merrier. You on, Ruth?"

Ruth patted her belly. "Sure. We like Mel Gibson, too."

Ari hadn't expected to have a good time, but she did. It had been years since she and Coe, only a year apart in age, had spent much time together. Russ, seven years older, had always seemed grown-up, doing grown-up male things and not interested in palling around with a little sister, although he'd always been kind, if somewhat bossy.

Joey and Jimmy had surprisingly decided to tag along to the movies with them, and imitating their childhood behavior, sat behind the couples, whispered comments and fought over popcorn.

Ari finally crept into her bed after midnight. After the movies they'd waited in line for ice cream, eating it out of waffle cones while they crossed the street, sat on the wall and watched the few remaining tourists at the Pier. Even when everyone drifted back to the cars parked on the other side of the Pier Village, Ari was comfortable with Max. "Thanks," she'd said.

He hadn't known what she was talking about. "For what?"

She'd shrugged, not knowing how to put it into words. Because somehow, in one lovely, rowdy, hot summer evening, she'd become part of the family again. She hadn't known how much she'd missed them or wanted that sense of belonging again.

Of course, it was nice to touch base, wonderful to reconnect. To know she could, like the telephone commercial sang, Reach Out and Touch Someone. It was good to have been reminded she was part of a family, no matter where she lived.

Montana. Just the sound of the word made Ari long for the Rockies and the wide, gorgeous expanse of plains that stretched west to the foothills. Ari climbed into her bed and pulled the sheet over her naked body.

The sticky humidity clung to her skin as she rearranged the sheet.

Montana. Cool, dry air and bright days without fog. Piles of snow in the winter, with a sharp wind from Canada that took her breath away when she trudged across campus to her office.

She tried to ignore the Rhode Island climate and to concentrate on winter in Bozeman, but Max's wonderful face intruded upon her thoughts. She almost wished she was back on the deck of the *Million*, stretched out beneath Max's hard body. But she was glad she hadn't done anything so foolish as make love to Max today.

There were only a few weeks left, and she had to keep her wits about her and her clothes on, no matter how much she longed to touch Max's pirate body.

ARI SURVEYED the collection of junk spread over the front lawn. "What masochist invented yard sales?"

"One with parents who haven't tossed anything out in over forty years," Coe answered.

"Now it all has a price." She sighed. "Everything's under fifty cents."

"Except Dad's golf clubs."

"Which he never used." Ari smiled. "Once a fisherman, always a—"

Ruth approached them. "I'm so glad it didn't rain." She frowned at the makeshift table her husband had put together with sawhorses and a piece of plywood. "Do you think that will hold up?"

Coe winced. "Have faith in me, woman."

"Not when you're supposed to be putting the cribs together this weekend."

"Yeah. I know I can do it. Russ said he'd come over and help me if I got in trouble."

"He's had enough exper . . ." Ari's voice trailed off as she watched a familiar truck pull up to the curb. Minutes later Max stepped across the lawn with two large boxes of doughnuts in his arms.

"Bless the man," Ruthie murmured. "Eight o'clock in the morning, and he brings food."

Ari's heart melted a little more. He'd offered to help, but she hadn't believed he'd really want to get involved with the Simones' pathetic version of a flea market. She walked across the moist lawn to greet him, and realized how glad she was to see him. He looked wonderful, in worn jeans and a thick beige cotton sweater. Ari suddenly felt shabby in her jeans, frayed sneakers and one of her brothers' old Narragansett High School sweatshirts.

"Here, sweetheart. Chocolate-covered, just as I promised," Max said, handing her one of the boxes. He stared at her lips for a moment, as if debating whether or not to kiss her in front of the entire Simone clan, then smiled instead. "Missed you last night," he murmured near her ear so only Ari could hear.

Ari was confused. Last night had been Friday and she hadn't made any plans with Max. "Why?"

But Joey interrupted when he came over and clapped Max on the shoulder. "Didn't expect to see you up this early, old man."

"Old man?" Ari laughed.

"It ended up being an early night." There was a warning in Max's voice that Joey didn't catch, but Ari heard the undertones and wondered what was going on. Where had they been last night? She'd priced junk all day long and had collapsed into her bed at nine-thirty.

"I did as I promised," Max said, turning back to Ari when Joey's attention was claimed by a rapidly waving Peggy.

"What's that?"

"I called one of the ladies who answered the ad." Max had a sheepish look on his face.

Ari didn't know whether to laugh, shout for joy or cry. So she didn't do anything, just looked at Max and waited. "And?"

He shrugged. "I met her at the Coast Guard House for drinks."

"And?"

"She has sixteen cats and eight dogs and told me their names and everything they do."

"Oh, Max."

"I'm an animal lover, really, but twenty-four devoted pets is too much for me. She was gorgeous, though, and a really nice woman."

"A veterinarian?" Ari fought jealousy, resolving to watch her pet intake in later years.

He shook his head. "Her assistant. I think she ends up with every stray animal that should have been put to sleep."

"Arianna!" Peggy's voice carried through the sultry morning air. "How much is this iron bed supposed to be? I think the sticker fell off."

"Coming," Ari called, trying to remember what price she'd stuck onto the old beast. If Max had answered one of the letters, that meant he'd changed his mind about the deal they'd made. Was it the letter she'd shoved into his jacket while she was on the boat last weekend? Suddenly she wondered what had happened to the rest of the letters. She turned to ask him, but Peggy came barreling across the lawn.

"People are already starting to come, and I don't think I have enough change," Peggy told her.

"I stuck some extra rolls of quarters and dimes in the drawer in the hutch," Ari assured her mother. "Want a doughnut?"

Peggy shook her head. "No time now, but you should put them in the kitchen, so people don't think they're for sale."

"Good idea."

Arianna touched Max's arm. "Want some coffee before this thing gets going?"

He shook his head. "I can't stay. I'll be back later, though. Don't make any plans for tonight."

"I may not make it until tonight," she muttered, watching car after car roll up to the curb in front of the house. She hadn't expected such a crowd for a simple yard sale, and wondered how disappointed people would be when they saw the quality of the stuff. "I may not make it until noon."

"Go hide in the kitchen and have a jelly doughnut," he offered.

"Will you come too?"

He looked at his watch. "Okay, but just for a minute. I have work stacked up at the plant."

"You're busy there, aren't you?"

Max nodded, following her into the kitchen. "The Japanese are big customers. Suddenly it's become an international company."

Ari poured herself a cup of coffee. Peggy had used the thirty-cup pot, clearly anticipating that her children would need help waking up on a Saturday morning. "Is that good?"

"Making money's always good. It's hard to keep up with all the work, though. Jerry's out this week—we really can't afford to keep the boat in the harbor."

"And you love being out on the sea, don't you?" Ari knew the answer before she asked.

He nodded. "Almost more than anything," he replied, touching her hair, pulling a curl. "Come here."

She shook her head. "Uh-uh. I have work to do."

He wrapped her in his arms anyway, kissing her soundly on the lips before he released her. "See you tonight," he said.

"I'll pick out another letter," she promised.

"Perhaps," Max said, his face expressionless. In two steps he was out the kitchen door, leaving Ari with a cup of steaming coffee and an opened box of chocolate doughnuts. She hadn't expected him to agree so quickly. Had he taken the veterinarian's assistant home to bed, despite the fact that she talked about her pets? A hot-blooded man could overlook a few problems in the heat of passion, couldn't he? Her brothers certainly had.

No, she didn't really think Max was a user, didn't think he made love to women indiscriminately just because they were there. Even thought a woman with all those pets must be a very kind, very caring and sympathetic person. Which was exactly what Max needed.

Ari eased a doughnut out of the box and comforted herself with the notion that she could get Max to tell her all about it tonight.

"Arianna, for heaven's sake!" Rusty entered the kitchen looking distraught.

"Hi, Dad. Want a doughnut?"

He shook his head. "Your mother's having a fit out there, and you're inside eating doughnuts?"

"I'm taking a break," she said mildly. "It's breakfast."

"But—" he sputtered.

"I priced everything, so all they have to do is take the money." Ari gestured at the kitchen door. "There are about six Simones out there helping. I didn't think they'd miss one more."

Rusty looked doubtful, then reached into the box and pried a doughnut away from the rest of the stack. "I saw the captain's car."

Ari nodded. "He just left."

"He's a good man," her father said, a warning in his voice. "Don't hurt him."

"How could I hurt Max?" Ari protested. "I've made it clear that I'm leaving in—" she thought quickly "—four weeks."

Rusty winced. "You could get a job here, at the college."

Ari didn't want to hurt her father's feelings. "Come on, Dad. Let's go see if they've sold your golf clubs yet."

"Darn things," he muttered. "Never could understand why your mother thought I wanted silly things like that."

Hours later, after the morning rush had eliminated two-thirds of the Simone leftovers, the only stuff remaining on the tables was either expensive or trash. Ari looked at the yard and began to consolidate tables, dismantling others, and throwing anything marked under twenty-five cents into a large plastic trash can.

The rest of the family disappeared, Ruthie and Coe to assemble the baby cribs, and the others off to who knows where. Peggy had hired someone to make chowder, but had driven down to the kitchen to make sure everything was going smoothly. The front yard was quiet, still littered with Simone possessions, like the scene of a battlefield bereft of soldiers. Ari didn't mind. It was good to keep busy. The sun was out and the humidity wasn't too terrible for a July afternoon. It was already after one o'clock. With the sale scheduled to end at three, the remaining two hours stretched before her. Ari leaned back in a lawn chair and stuck her nose into a paperback book. She'd finished rereading Jane Austen and had now switched to Regencies written by modern authors. Ari soon became entranced by the story of a young woman's introduction to London society, so the afternoon went quickly. A young couple bought the old kitchen set, eager to scrape the paint away and see the wood underneath. Ari wished them luck and took their offer of twenty dollars. Some neighborhood kids bought an old Polaroid camera and a couple of very used orange Frisbees.

Ari ate a bowl of chowder and a couple of dough- nuts for lunch, polishing off two cans of diet cola and one more book before the afternoon was done. She dumped the unsold merchandise into the trash and wondered what Max was doing right now. Had he got- ten more mail? Had he picked out the letter from the animal lover, or was it one she'd shoved at him last week? What did the women say when they wrote to the mysterious post office box? Had Max read them all?

Her father strolled outside and looked around. He handed her a long white envelope. "For you," he said. "From Montana."

Ari took it and looked at the postmark. It had been forwarded, to be sure, but had been mailed from Nar- ragansett. Ari thought the name on the return address was familiar, but wasn't sure. She slit the flap open and unfolded a bright red piece of paper.

The fifteenth high school reunion announcement stared back at her, its neat hand-printed letters shout- ing Hurrah! across the top of the page.

Hurrah? She read on.

Sorry for the short notice, but we never were a very organized class and since we missed getting together for the tenth, some of us thought the fif- teenth was too good a year to pass up for a party!

So come one, come all to the Narragansett Inn Lounge, Friday, August 3, 7:00 p.m. for an infor-

mal party. See old friends and catch up on the
years since we graduated!

Ari wondered whether it would be worth the effort.
"What is it, hon?"

She folded the paper and stuck it back into the envelope. "An invitation to the high school reunion."

"Oh, that's right. I think your mother gave them your
address a few months ago. They having a get-together?"

"Yes. Nothing special."

"Well, that's nice." He patted her back. "You need to
get out more, look up some of your old friends."

"I'll see." Ari didn't have the heart to tell him that
there was no one to look up. Liz lived in Maine, Katie
in Pennsylvania. She didn't think either woman, occupied with busy families, would have the time or the
interest. She couldn't think of anyone she wanted to
catch up on old times with.

Her father interrupted her thoughts. "How much
money did we make today?"

Ari was grateful for the change of subject. "Last time
I counted, we'd hit the three-hundred-dollar mark."

He grinned, his red beard shaking with laughter.
"No!"

"It's true." She smiled back at him. "You didn't know
how much good junk you had, did you?"

"As long as you got rid of those golf clubs, I don't
mind."

"I did." She sat down on the bench at the picnic table
and looked around. "It's after five. I should put the tables away. I'm exhausted."

"The boys will be home soon. I'll make them do it,"
Rusty offered. "You've done enough. You should go
take a swim."

"That's not a bad idea," she said, glad to leave the yard and go inside to change. Cold ocean water might be just what she needed to quit feeling sorry for herself. Ari pulled on her yellow suit, tossed a large T-shirt over it, picked up the car keys and a towel. Her father was busy helping himself to chowder from the pot simmering on the stove when Ari came back into the kitchen. "I'll be back in half an hour. I might grab a sandwich, too. You want anything?"

He shook his head. "I thought you were going out with the captain tonight."

She wished her family wouldn't call him the captain. "Well, if he calls, tell him I'll be back at six."

Rusty nodded, pleased to have been entrusted with the message. "Ayuh, I'll tell the man. He'll be calling, you know."

Maybe, Ari thought. Maybe he was answering another letter. Which was what she wanted, she reminded herself. What she had set up herself. She'd have to get over these childish, jealous feelings, that was all.

She was on the beach in less than ten minutes. Ari loved Narragansett at this hour, when it was practically empty. The mothers and children had gone home for dinner, the surfers had finally exhausted themselves, and the teenage girls were baked to a crisp and off to jobs or dates. Ari curled her toes in the warm sand and looked at the smooth expanse of ocean. The water would still be warm, the wind was down to nothing, and the sky was a gorgeous purply pink and blue smear. Another hour and it would be too chilly, so Ari tossed her belongings onto the sand and strolled into the surf, enjoying the way the waves hit her ankles and splashed against her calves.

She'd missed this, she admitted to herself. It was the same as the summer when she'd been sixteen and crazily in love with Eddie Barton. She'd head down here to the Pier after work in the Dairy Queen and rinse off the stickiness of six hours of making hot fudge sundaes and ice-cream cones. Ari gazed around—it looked like this fifteen years ago. It felt like this fifteen years ago, except now her body had more curves than bones. Her hair was shorter and curlier, her heart heavier. Wiser.

Ari mentally shook herself out of the blues and dived into the next wave, slipping under its breaking crest to appear on the other side of the swell. She shook her bangs from her eyes as she paddled sideways and watched the shore. Although the waves were big enough for bodysurfing, she was content to stay inside the breakwater. She swam with long overarm strokes and dived under the swells when she felt like it. Ari felt her spirits lift. It had been a long time since she'd played in the water.

She wiped the water from her face and looked toward the shore. A tall man stood by the mound of clothing she'd left on the sand. Max—it could only be Max—waved to her. Ari hesitated, then waved back. He stripped the shirt from his chest and tossed it to the sand, then kicked off his loafers. The bathing suit was black and looked like shorts at first. Ari was relieved—she couldn't picture Max in those revealing bikinis men wore these days. He walked quickly through the surf, then dived, as Ari had, to appear a few yards away.

Ari trod water, keeping her shoulders out of the rapidly cooling air to stay warm. Max looked wonderful, his dark hair streaming from his forehead until he slicked it back with a graceful motion and a shake of his head. Ari felt as if she were losing her breath and wondered if she'd been in the water too long. In three strokes he was beside her, and the brief brush of his slick shoulder against her arm was oddly erotic.

"You knew I was here?"

"Your father told me when I called." He pointed past the beach to the row of town houses that faced the water. "I live over there. It was a simple matter of picking up the binoculars. By the way, I told him I'd be meeting you at the beach and taking you out to dinner."

"In my bathing suit?"

"An informal meal."

"I didn't know you lived in the village."

"For a year now." He grinned and brushed water from her cheek. "You're welcome anytime."

"Thanks. I've always wondered what those places looked like from inside. They must be beautiful."

"I have a view of beautiful women swimming in my front yard."

"Lucky guy."

Max grinned. "I've always thought so."

"Why are you here?"

"To find you." He drifted closer, his hair-roughened leg touching hers as she stood up to her chin in water. "Any objections?"

She felt the heat of his body through the narrow band of water that separated them. Why had she thought swimming alone was fun? This was definitely more intriguing than bodysurfing. "None that I can think of."

"Good." Max put his arms around her, his hands slipping easily along her back through the salt water. Her breasts touched his bare chest, sending erotic little ripples through her body. The gentle motion of the water rocked her against his hard chest, and Ari kicked her feet as the swell knocked her from a standing position. When she was able to stand again, the lower half of her body brushed against his abdomen, and Ari felt the evidence that Max wanted her. It was an intriguing and powerful feeling, and although Ari tried to avoid brushing against him, she couldn't, because the grip of his arms around her back had slid to her waist, and the gentle swell of waves competed with her attempts to avoid the intimate parts of Max's body.

"Excuse me," she muttered, embarrassed. She really wanted to put her mouth to his smooth shoulder and taste the salt. She wanted to lick his collarbone, trace the hard ridge with her tongue. She wanted—

"No," he growled and thrust her away, his hands releasing her waist and tossing her back a few inches.

"What?"

"If you're going to seduce me, it won't be for a quick two minutes in the ocean."

"Two minutes?"

He grimaced. "Your sliding around like that is dangerous."

"You were the one doing the sliding around. You grabbed *me*. It wasn't the other way around."

"I was hanging on to you so you wouldn't drown."

"I wasn't—" She stopped when she saw him laugh and realized he'd been teasing her. Tired of struggling to tread water, Ari swam toward the beach so she could touch the sandy ocean floor.

"Going in?"

"No," she said as he followed her. "I want to stand up."

"You can curl your legs around me," he offered. "You can put your hands around my neck and hang on."

"And what will you be doing?"

"Using my imagination," Max said on a sigh as he reached to curl a hand around her waist. He tugged her toward him. "I love feeling your skin under the water."

Ari knew she was asking for trouble, but the warm water and the cool night sent goose bumps along her skin wherever it was exposed to the air. She didn't struggle when he pulled her against him. "Maybe this isn't such a good idea," she began hesitantly.

"Too late," he growled, smoothing his palms along her bare back. She felt him against her again and wanted to melt around him.

The water, she told herself. She could blame it on the water, the slick skin and invisible body parts and the salt....

His hands skimmed to her shoulders and he slipped the straps down her arms.

"Max," she warned, but her voice was weak. She couldn't ever remember such an erotic experience and wanted to see what he'd do next. If she could only taste his skin. She licked her lips, tasting the salty water and looked at him as drops of water trickled down his face, ran over his shoulders and touched hers. His fingers traced a line across the bathing-suit bodice and dipped inside.

"Max," she said, wanting to stop him. "Quit teasing like this."

"I'm not teasing," he said. "I want to feel your breasts against me." He tugged the bodice down, freeing her breasts in the warm water, and Ari gasped with pleasure as her nipples touched the scratchy mat of chest hair. Max claimed her mouth then, crushing her to him and parting her lips with his tongue. Ari opened willingly, needing to feel him, to taste him, to press her suddenly boneless body against his. It was a plunging, reckless kiss, and it claimed them both for a long, long moment.

When Max finally lifted his head, Ari clung to his slick shoulders, glad he held on to her. Without his grasp she would have drifted out to sea like some spineless mermaid or a jellyfish. Max held her tightly, letting her brush against him as he traced a trail of kisses along her throat, lifted the heavy, wet hair from her neck and licked salty drops of water off her skin.

"Come home with me," he demanded.

"I can't," she lied.

"You can shower and change."

Ari didn't have anything to change into, but she knew that wasn't the point. Max wasn't asking her to come home with him so she could clean up. "I shouldn't."

"Why not?"

"A one-night affair?"

He lifted his mouth from her skin and looked into her eyes. "That's not what I'm asking for. That's never been what I've asked for."

"I know." Ari sighed, knowing the truth of his words. "But that's the only way it could be."

He shook his head. "We're better than that."

"It wouldn't be fair."

"It wouldn't be fair if you left."

Ari felt the chill on her shoulders as the sun dipped lower. She quickly wriggled her bathing-suit top into place. "There's no law that says life is fair."

He frowned. "You're not talking to one of your nephews, Ari. I've wanted you since that day on Block Island, and you know it."

She didn't try to deny it. "I've tried to be honest."

He shook his head, his eyes dark and serious. "Uh-uh, sweetheart. You were being honest when you kissed me. Refusing to see what's right in front of your eyes is denying reality."

Anger shot through her, and she felt she needed to defend herself. "*Reality?* Or just sex?"

"Not true."

"What then?" She ran a shaking hand across his chest. "Surely not love."

The expression on his face remained impassive. "No?" At her silence he added, "Why not?"

"You don't fall in love in one day. Or two."

"I did."

Her hand dropped from his skin and she stepped back out of his embrace. It was difficult to walk through the heavy ocean swells despite the fact there there was little surf, but Ari turned away from the comfort of Max's body and headed to the beach.

"Running away?" he called. Those were the only two words Ari heard as she arched her body to catch a small swell and rode the wave to shore. She coasted, feeling her belly scratch the sandy bottom as she opened her eyes. The ride had lasted only a moment, but it was fun. She'd forgotten how much she used to enjoy stretching out in front of a wave, waiting for just the right moment. Then, arms extended and face down, she'd let the wave carry her to shore. Once she'd scrambled to her feet and caught her breath, she'd head back out to do it all over again.

But now ocean water clogged her throat. Ari coughed and scrambled to her feet. Max's large hand reached out to steady her and she tried not to notice his strong, brown legs in the black trunks or the thick chest just waiting for her to put her face against it and burrow her face into the hollow in his shoulder.

Ari grabbed her towel.

"You're freezing," he said from behind her.

She wrapped the towel around her shoulders and pushed the wet hair from her brow. She picked a sliver of seaweed from her wrist before she looked at Max. He'd pulled a T-shirt over his head and she watched the wet spots expand across the material. "Not really," she argued, but she didn't feel much like arguing anymore.

Max sensed it. "Come on. My place is right across the street. You won't have to drive home wet and sandy. While you're taking a shower, I'll order dinner." When Ari still looked doubtful, he reassured her. "No seduction, just pizza, I promise."

It made her smile. Max felt relief so thick it almost choked him. He stepped closer and took her small hand into his, then waited while she bent to grab the rest of her belongings with the other hand. She scooped up his shoes, too, and they walked down the beach like old friends, successfully avoiding the leftover sand castles and the holes children, trying to reach some mysterious destination only they knew of, had dug in the sand.

THEY JOINED the crowds of tourists doing some window-shopping before climbing the outside stairs to Max's home. He unlocked the door and let Ari step inside.

"I hope I don't track sand all over your carpet," she said when she saw the beige color of the carpet stretching from one white wall to another.

"It's not a problem," he said. "That's why I picked that color. Just go on in."

The windows were large and wide, and filled with the view of the ocean and the seawall. "This is gorgeous," she said, realizing the luxurious living room held only

NO RISK, NO OBLIGATION
TO BUY...NOW OR EVER!

GUARANTEED

PLAY "ROLL A DOUBLE"
AND GET AS MANY AS SIX GIFTS!

HERE'S HOW TO PLAY:

1. Peel off label from front cover. Place it in space provided at right. With a coin, carefully scratch off the silver dice. This makes you eligible to receive one or more free books, and possibly other gifts, depending on what is revealed beneath the scratch-off area.

2. You'll receive brand-new Harlequin Temptation® novels. When you return this card, we'll rush you the books and gifts you qualify for ABSOLUTELY FREE!

3. Then, if we don't hear from you, every month we'll send you 4 additional novels to read and enjoy. You can return them and owe nothing, but if you decide to keep them, you'll pay only $2.39 per book—a savings of 56¢ each off the cover price.

4. When you subscribe to the Harlequin Reader Service®, you'll also get our newsletter, as well as additional free gifts from time to time.

5. You must be completely satisfied. You may cancel at any time simply by sending us a note or a shipping statement marked ''cancel'' or by returning any shipment to us at our expense.

You'll look like a million dollars when you wear this elegant necklace! It's a generous 20 inches long and each link is double-soldered for strength and durability.

"ROLL A DOUBLE!"

PLACE LABEL HERE

SCRATCH HERE

SEE CLAIM CHART BELOW

142 CIH ACJ5

YES! I have placed my label from the front cover into the space provided above and scratched off the silver dice. Please rush me the free book(s) and gift(s) that I am entitled to. I understand that I am under no obligation to purchase any books, as explained on the opposite page.

NAME _____

ADDRESS _____ APT. _____

CITY _____ STATE _____ ZIP CODE _____

CLAIM CHART

	4 FREE BOOKS PLUS FREE 20" NECKLACE PLUS MYSTERY BONUS GIFT
	3 FREE BOOKS PLUS BONUS GIFT
	2 FREE BOOKS

CLAIM NO. 37-829

HARLEQUIN "NO RISK" GUARANTEE

- You're not required to buy a single book—ever!
- You must be completely satisfied or you may cancel at any time simply by sending us a note or a shipping statement marked "cancel" or by returning any shipment to us at our cost. Either way, you will receive no more books; you'll have no obligation to buy.
- The free book(s) and gift(s) you claimed on this "Roll A Double" offer remain yours to keep no matter what you decide.

If offer card is missing, please write to:
Harlequin Reader Service, 3010 Walden Ave., P.O. Box 1867, Buffalo, N.Y. 14269-1867

a few pieces of furniture. "How long have you lived here?"

"Only a year."

She stepped farther into the living room and admired a huge seascape on the wall before she noticed the hat. "That's the hat I lost on the ferry!" she exclaimed, picking it up off the glass coffee table.

Max stepped beside her. "This is a replacement. I bought it at Woolworth's, but I've always forgotten to bring it with me." He didn't tell her he'd forgotten it on purpose, preferring to see her hat lying on the table as if she lived there and would return any minute to put it on and run away with him. It reminded him of silk dresses and weddings.

"You didn't have to bother." She started to put it back onto the table, but Max took it from her.

"I wanted to," he murmured, setting the wide-brimmed hat on Ari's head. "I dreamed of us making love while you wore nothing but this hat and those long earrings."

Ari pretended his words had no effect on her. "Pretty kinky for a fisherman."

He shrugged. "Those long nights at sea are tough. I'd be happy to share a few other ideas with you."

"No, thanks." But she smiled. She liked him better when he teased and joked around. At least then she could pretend that Maximilian Cole's presence in her life was nothing more than a pleasant interlude in an otherwise family-filled summer.

Too much family.

Too much Max.

He touched her face, tracing a line with his finger. She thought he would dip his head under the wide brim of the hat, but he didn't. Instead he straightened and plucked the hat from her head as easily as he had placed it. Ari felt a disappointed pang and firmly told herself it was for the best.

"Come on," he said. I'll show you where the bathroom is."

Along the way she peeked into a large white-walled room, her attention caught again by the windows that showcased the sea. A king-size bed took up most of the space, its puffy comforter printed with green, white and cream triangles. Several polished, antique dressers stood in the room producing an intriguing combination of styles.

Max saw her look. "My grandmother's," he said, pointing to the oak furniture. He motioned toward a half-open door around the corner. "There's a Jacuzzi in my bathroom, if you'd like to try it. Otherwise there's a guest bath down the hall."

"The guest bath is fine," she said. The place was immaculate for a bachelor's. She watched as he swung open a hall door, revealing a bathroom decorated in cream with white fixtures. He rummaged through a narrow closet and pulled out two towels. "Everything you need should be in here. My sisters have left all sorts of things here in the cupboard."

Sisters. Did he think she would believe that?

He grinned. "It's true. I'll show you their pictures after we eat."

Ari thanked him and was glad to shut the door and gain a few minutes to herself so she could compose her thoughts. All right, she was thirty-two years old. She'd been in men's apartments.

But this was Max. This was different. This was a man who looked at her with an expression she hadn't seen before. It was a look that said, *You're mine, whether you know it or not.*

Well, she didn't know it. Wouldn't accept such a thing. Would fly off into the sunset in a few short weeks, on August 27, no matter what.

After the reunion.

After her parents were settled.

Before the first faculty meeting on August 31.

Ari struggled to peel the wet suit from her body. Her knees still felt weak from the desire Max had aroused while they were swimming. It could be from hunger, she argued. Nevertheless, she'd have to be careful and never go swimming with him again. It had been an entirely too sensual experience.

She turned on the faucets and adjusted the temperature before stepping into the hot stream of water and pulling the shower curtain shut. *You don't fall in love in one day,* she'd told him.

Liar.

For the first year since she'd started teaching, Ari didn't look forward to going back to class.

7

ARI TOOK a quick shower. She stepped out of the tub
and grabbed the towel she'd left folded beside the sink.
The casual intimacy of standing naked in Max's apartment was strangely comfortable.

She didn't want to get too comfortable. Ari decided
it would be better to stay edgy and get out fast.

Max rapped once on the bathroom door. "Do you
want a robe?"

"Uh, no thanks." Prancing through his house in
nothing but a robe didn't seem like a very smart idea.

"Well, you can't walk around in a towel," he muttered, and then there was silence. Though Ari didn't like
the idea, she'd have to rinse the ocean water from her
bathing suit and put it back on, then shake the sand out
of her T-shirt. Ari dried her hair, found a comb in a
drawer and worked it through the tangles. She was glad
Max's sisters—whoever they were—had left shampoo
and conditioner in a holder on the shower head.

"Here," Max's voice came through the door. "Try
these."

She checked to make sure the towel was wrapped securely around her and opened the door. Max stood
there with a small bundle of clothes in his hands. "I
don't wear these, but I understand this is the fashion,"
he said, a twinkle in his blue eyes.

Ari took the clothes. "Thanks."

She shut the door and looked at what he'd brought her. Two pairs of brand-new men's paisley boxer shorts, still packaged in their plastic bags. Max was right. She'd seen her students wear two pairs of the boxer shorts, one over the other, rolled up at the hem. Interesting. The other was a brilliant red T-shirt proclaiming the superiority of the University of Nebraska football team. She put the clothes on and felt about fifteen years old. It seemed to be the recurring theme of the summer, only this time she didn't mind too much. She was glad her legs were slim from climbing stairs at home, and wondered absently if Max entertained much. Again, the thought of sisters made her wish she knew more about him.

When she left the guest bath, Ari heard the water running in his bathroom; the bedroom door was open and his wet bathing suit lay crumpled on the carpet. Ari went downstairs, afraid he'd shut off the water and walk nude into the bedroom. Why would he be used to shutting doors?

She wondered if he'd ordered pizza and assumed he had. He always did what he said he would, didn't he? He wasn't a man who broke promises, at least none that she knew of.

She strolled through the living room, peeking at the books on the shelves. The man liked mysteries, spy stories and Stephen King. You had to be brave to read Stephen King, Ari thought. She'd never been able to make it through one of his books without being scared to death.

Because she lived alone.

She poked around shamelessly, noticed the high school yearbooks in the bookcase, on the bottom shelf, and pulled one from its place. She flipped through it, wondering what the eighteen-year-old Max would look like. The class of '69's yearbook was bright red with a Confederate flag attached to the cover to feature the South Kingstown Rebels. Ari flipped through the pictures of the senior class and found Max. His hair was parted to one side, his eyes were steady and calm. He seemed comfortable, a hint of a smile edging his lips. It was a familiar expression. She glanced at his name in the column on the right-hand side of the page and saw that his middle name was Lloyd, his course in school was College, Future Intentions was listed as College, his favorite pastimes were football, basketball and—

"Find anything interesting?"

Ari looked up to see Max, shirtless and barefoot, wearing only hip-hugging jeans. "Just wondering what you looked like in 1969."

He grimaced. "You'll never love me now."

Love him? Ari decided not to answer that statement. "I was just getting to the part about Activities."

"I can't remember." He walked up to her and looked over her shoulder at the opened book. "Football team, basketball team and junior prom committee," he read.

"That doesn't tell me much," she said, inhaling the scent of piney soap and one very clean male body. His bare chest was perilously close to her shoulder. Her T-shirt felt thin and Ari wished she was wearing a bra— an ironclad bra that would protect her from the delicious sensation of his skin brushing against the cotton fabric.

"What do you want to know?" He moved away, and Ari was disappointed.

"Nothing in particular." She sighed. "I got an invitation to my fifteenth reunion today and I suppose I was curious about yearbooks. I don't even know where mine is." She pictured the two large boxes in her bedroom and thought she had a pretty good idea.

"My twentieth was last year. It was great. You'll have a good time."

"I don't think I'm going to go."

He looked surprised as he took the book out of her hands, tossed it onto the coffee table and brushed her shoulders with his wide, strong palms. "Why not?"

Because my boyfriend died and I don't think I can deal with the memories, even fifteen years later. The words remained lodged in her throat and she avoided Max's curious gaze. "What's the point?"

"You get connected somehow," he said softly. "And you have a lot of laughs and see how people grew up." He touched her face with one finger. "You grew up beautiful."

She made a face. "Thank you for thinking that, but—"

"No buts," he countered. "You should go."

"I'll think about it."

"When is it?"

"Next weekend, but I just found out about it today."

"They didn't give you much notice."

"The invitation went to Montana first."

Max studied her face. Closed, as if the secrets she wanted to protect were safely tucked out of sight. Didn't she realize that when she tried to hide her feelings, it showed as if a glaring neon arrow pointed to her embarrassment? Russ would be able to tell him why his little sister avoided fishing boats and didn't want to go to her reunion. But Max didn't want her brother to tell him. He wanted Ari to tell him herself, so he let her off the hook. "I ordered pizza. And a couple of spinach pies."

Ari's mouth watered. "I love spinach pies."

He grinned. "I thought you might."

"Why?"

He shrugged. "Just a hunch," he fibbed. Peggy Simone had said so once. *Take her out for a nice spinach pie or two*, had been her exact words. If Peggy had any more advice, Max resolved to follow it. He knew an ally when he saw one.

"Thanks for the clothes."

"You look good," he said. Good enough to peel the clothes away and take her upstairs to bed.

She pulled at the baggy material of the underwear. "Your sisters gave you these?"

He nodded. "I think it was a joke, but I'm not sure."

Ari decided she didn't want to discuss underwear styles with Max, especially since she was wearing his underwear and not her own. She turned to the living room and looked around helplessly for something else to talk about.

"We could talk about the weather," he offered.

She turned back to see that familiar smile on his face. "We could."

"Or," he added, "we could talk about our next trip to Block Island."

"Oh?" She didn't mind when he stepped closer and took her into his arms. She should mind, she knew. She should make excuses and hotfoot it across the street, run through the parking lot and drive sixty miles an hour all the way home. But she didn't move. His hands were warm as they encircled her waist. Damn, if only he didn't know she was naked underneath the silly boxer shorts and T-shirt. "I, uh, didn't know you'd want to go back."

"I always want to go back." He pressed closer to her as he tightened his embrace. "Only this time—"

The door bell buzzed, interrupting his words.

"The pizza," she suggested softly, trying to regain her breath.

"Damn," he said, releasing her. "Guess your virtue is safe until after dinner."

"You're still hung up on my virtue?" She followed him to the door. She had a terrific view of his broad, brown back and thought if anyone's virtue was in danger, it just might be Max Cole's. She liked backs. Liked strong shoulders. Liked to rub her fingers along the ridge of spine and run her tongue along the intriguing angles of shoulder blades....

"I hope you're hungry," Max said. He reached into his jeans pocket for his wallet as he opened the door.

Ari sighed. She was an idiot. A fool. There were only a few weeks left of her summer, and going to bed with Max wasn't part of the vacation package. He wasn't a compromising man, she knew—he lived his life his own way and if anyone wanted to accept that, that was fine with him.

There would be no compromises, no long, long-distance relationship. She wouldn't allow herself to fall in love with a seafaring man once again. She was not going to risk tossing her heart out to sea and waiting for the tide to return it.

Ari watched Max take the pizza, topped with a closed white bag, into his hands—those strong, capable-looking hands—and shut the door. When his gaze met Ari's, she steeled herself for the accompanying swell of desire and tried not to show how she felt.

This was getting ridiculous, Max decided. He'd give her dinner and send her home. He was growing tired of playing games. The stack of unopened mail in the corner of the dining room only annoyed him—visible proof that Ari didn't want him, that she was willing to hand him over to somebody else, like a used sofa at the Simone yard sale.

"What's the matter?"

"Nothing," he said, shaking his head.

"You looked upset."

"The box is burning my fingers." He turned and strode into the kitchen, not waiting to see if she'd follow him. She did, because he could smell the scent of flowers. *Must be the shampoo*, he decided. He wanted to take her into his arms and make love to her for a few hours. Hell, a few days might be more like it.

Would she be out of his system then? he wondered. Would he be able to board the *Million* and sail off into the sunset afterward?

Or would he hang around like a sea gull on the docks, grateful for any scrap of garbage that came his way? Max frowned as he set the warm box on the counter. The smell coming from it did little to lift his spirits. He'd hoped that a hot meal would take his mind off ravishing the beautiful woman who had come up beside him to peer at the pizza container.

"Aren't you going to open it?" she asked.

He flipped the top to reveal a pizza piled with every topping imaginable and heard Ari sigh with pleasure. "I'll get some plates. There's soda in the refrigerator. Help yourself," he said gruffly. By the time he'd grabbed silverware and plates, Ari had taken a can of diet cola to the butcher block table and paused to look out the window at the tourists below.

"You must have a store underneath this, right?"

"Yeah," he said, moving the food to the center of the table. He didn't have place mats. Would she mind?

"What kind?"

"I lease to a souvenir shop." He grabbed a shirt from the back of a chair and shrugged into it, absently buttoning enough to hold it together. "Come eat," he ordered, admiring the backs of her thighs as she stood at the window. Cute knees, too. He wondered if she was ticklish. "You can start with pizza or spinach pie. Your choice."

She turned away from the window and joined him at the small table. Her bare knees briefly brushed against denim as she sat down across from him. "Spinach pie."

"Don't you want a glass? Ice?"

"This is fine," she said, setting the can of cola to one side and reaching eagerly for the bag. Food was exactly what she needed to take her mind off sex.

IT WORKED for a while, but unfortunately didn't last forever. Ari helped Max clean up the kitchen, but that only meant the brief chores of putting silverware into the dishwasher and throwing everything else into the garbage. They'd eaten every bite of food.

"Next time I invite you to dinner, remind me to order extra," Max commented.

"Okay," she agreed, once again standing in front of the open window and looking out at the ocean. The breeze was heavy with the smell of the sea. "What a beautiful evening."

"Want to go for a walk?" He went to her and looked over her shoulder at the pinkening sky.

"Red sky in morning," she began, in the singsong manner of the familiar phrase.

"Sailor take warning," he finished for her. "Red sky at night . . ."

"Sailor's delight," she murmured, still watching the horizon. He put a gentle hand upon her shoulders and rubbed. No bra straps impeded his caress, the smooth cotton of his T-shirt slipped easily over Ari's skin, and Max ached to hold her in his arms. But he'd promised her no seduction, and he intended to be a man of his word. His fingertips regretfully squeezed her upper arms before he stepped away from the fragrant scent of her hair.

"Want to go for a walk?"

She turned, an embarrassed look on her face. "I don't think I have enough clothes on."

"Two pairs of underwear and a solid red shirt?"

She nodded. "It feels a little strange."

"You're in New England now, hon—in a resort town. Don't you remember running around the Pier in your bikini when you were a teenager?"

"That was a long time ago."

"And a very small bikini."

"How do you know that?"

"Everyone wore small bikinis," he said, smiling at the memory. "It was torture and heaven at the same time for a teenage boy, you know."

"Where are we walking?"

"We'll go below and window-shop. I'll buy you ice cream. Or frozen yogurt."

"The place with the waffle cones?" He nodded. "Then you're on. Let me get my sandals."

Max held her hand as they strolled along the sidewalk. The evening air was still warm, although it was almost eight o'clock. There was a line in front of the movie theater and across the street, at an exclusive

Spanish restaurant, gaily dressed people hovered near the entrance. Ari paused in front of the souvenir shop's window.

"Looking for something to take back to Montana with you?"

Ari shook her head. "No, I don't think so."

"Don't you want any reminders of Rhode Island?"

His voice sounded almost bitter. It surprised Ari, and she looked at him, trying to figure out what his expression meant.

"I have enough," she said. *And it will hurt to leave you*, she wanted to add. She wanted to lean into his strength, wanted him to take away her loneliness and make love to her. Ari didn't stop to question why, but knew she was in danger of falling in love with Max. And it could only mean trouble for both of them.

"All right," he said easily. "Then let's walk."

He continued to hold her hand and they strolled along the crowded sidewalk, studying the tourists as much as the store windows. When Ari paused in front of a women's clothing shop with an exclusive air, Max tugged her through the open doorway. The smell of lavender surrounded them.

"What are you doing?" she protested, noting the obviously expensive clothes decorating the dusty-pink walls. "I didn't bring any money with me."

"I'm going to buy a souvenir for you," he said, a mischievous twinkle in his eyes. When the clerk asked if she could help them with anything, Max replied, "Yes. Lingerie."

The sophisticated-looking woman raised one eyebrow and tossed her long blond hair off her shoulders while she studied her latest customer. "Do you have anything, um, specific in mind?"

She'll be asking if he wants her to model for him next.
Ari tightened her grip on Max's hand. "Max!" Ari protested in a whisper.

"Underwear," he growled.

The woman smiled and pointed a long red fingernail toward a wicker chair, next to which stood a large basket filled with colorful scraps of silk. "Why don't you see if there's anything there that might interest you?"

Max dropped Ari's hand to walk over to the basket, where he explored the wispy undergarments as if he was combing through his fishing net. "What size?"

She knew he'd badger her until he found out, so she said. "Six."

"Good." He held up a pair of white bikini pants that were ninety-nine percent lace. "What do you think?"

"They're not very practical. And you're not buying me underwear."

"You just finished complaining about wearing mine." He looked pointedly at the boxer shorts. So did the saleswoman.

"It's the fashion, I suppose—" the saleswoman sniffed "—among teenagers."

Ari felt naked. Now all three of them knew she wasn't wearing any underwear. It wasn't as if her body parts were going to fall out of the baggy shorts, for heaven's sake. She would go back to Max's, find a clothes dryer, dry her bathing suit and go home. Then what? Sit around an empty house and watch reruns on television? "Just take me home, Max. I have plenty of underwear there."

"Not like this, I'll bet," he said, holding up a pair of pale peach panties edged with wide matching lace. "Your color." He looked at the dangling tag. "Your size, too."

When she didn't answer, Max took them to the counter and the saleswoman rang up the purchase, while Ari pretended the whole scene wasn't happening. She peeked at the price on an intricately embroidered cotton skirt and decided to wait outside rather than be tempted by the gorgeous clothes. Max followed her in a minute, his large fingers clutching a paper bag imprinted with a rose design.

"Last time you bought me a toothbrush and a hairbrush."

"Does this mean we're spending the night together again?" he asked.

She could only laugh at him. "Not on your life, sweetie."

"Then how about ice cream?"

Ari nodded and reached for his hand. "That I'll accept. But I don't know what you're going to do with the underwear in that package."

"Oh, yes, I do," Max said softly. His hand tightened around hers. "Someday I'm going to take them off you."

Ari felt a surprising jolt rush through her body that took her breath away. It wasn't easy to stand patiently in line at the ice-cream counter while pretending to decide what flavor to order, even though Chunk of Peach was her favorite. Here she stood in the middle of a cheerful summer crowd, while a man she was stupidly falling in love with held a bag that contained sexy underpants he intended to take off her someday in the not too distant future.

It was tempting. But if she didn't put them on, he couldn't take them off.

That was supposed to be comforting?

"I'm not going to wear them," she told him, when she caught his questioning look.

"You don't have to." His lips threatened to smile. "I only asked you what flavor ice cream you wanted."

"Oh."

"Well?"

"Peach." In another minute he handed her a cone of rapidly melting ice cream wrapped in a paper napkin, and Ari quickly licked the melting parts to keep the drops from overflowing the large waffle cone. The place was stifling and she was glad to make her way through the crowd and get into the fresh air again.

"How's yours?"

Ari offered it to him. "Want a taste?"

He ducked and took a bite from the side. "Not bad," he murmured. "Want some of mine?"

She looked at the dark mixture in his cone. "What is it?"

"Passion for Chocolate."

"No, thanks. I don't like chocolate that much, but what's in it?"

"Chocolate-covered peanuts and fudge."

Ari shook her head. "It's all yours." They walked back along the sidewalk and around the bend toward the souvenir shop. Ari knew she should be heading home. She wished she had her belongings with her, wished she hadn't left her purse in Max's living room. She would rather cross the street and head toward the parking lot and her car. It was the coward's way out, she knew, but she was allowed to wimp out occasionally, wasn't she? She followed Max up the stairs once more, desperately trying to finish her ice-cream cone and still look ladylike.

"Want something cold to drink?" Max asked after unlocking the door and gesturing for her to enter.

"No, I should go."

"You haven't asked me about the latest batch of responses to your ad."

"I saw the pile on the floor."

"I haven't opened them." He shut the door and sighed. "Are you going to pick out the suitable ones again?"

"Do you want me to?"

"Not especially."

Ari followed him into the kitchen and watched him toss the remainder of his ice-cream cone into the garbage. A ridiculous feeling of relief swept over her, and she tried to ignore it. How could she be happy that he still wanted her? He'd made that very clear a little while ago at the beach, when his hands had swept over her breasts and his mouth had taken hers. All right, so maybe she liked him too much. What would happen if they made love, if she gave in to every single impulse and desire she'd tried so hard to ignore . . . ?

Max stepped closer, letting the paper bag he'd held fall onto the carpet. "Ari?"

"What?"

"Come upstairs with me."

"You promised not to seduce me, remember?"

"I promised you pizza. You had pizza."

"A man of your word," she teased, wanting to touch him.

"Yes," he said. "But you could seduce me instead, sweetheart."

She wanted to, she really did; her knees grew watery just at the sound of the sexy growl of his voice and the tempting offer in his words. "For one time? Is that what you really want?" His expression didn't change, so Ari continued. "Because my life's not here, Max. In a few weeks I go back to the real world and this . . . will be over. I don't want either one of us to get hurt."

He clutched her shoulders and bent down to look into her eyes. "I'll take the chance."

"Max—"

His cold lips touched hers and Ari thought her heart had stopped. When he finally lifted his head he added, "and I'll make you change your mind."

That was impossible, Ari stubbornly thought, but he kissed her again, and the heat trailed through her body. She clung to his waist for support while his tongue delved and played and sent erotic messages to other sensitized parts of her body.

"Upstairs," he murmured. "I've dreamed of you naked in my bed."

"I'm not naked yet," she tried to tease, but the words sounded more like a complaint, even in her own ears.

"I have a solution," he said lovingly, touching a nipple through the cotton fabric of her T-shirt. "It might take a while."

"Don't feel like you have to hurry on my account," Ari whispered. Her breath caught in her throat at the look in his eyes. He wanted her and he wanted her to know how much. With words—he hadn't pressed his hard body against her. Ari wanted to slide her hand down his chest past the ridge of denim waistband to feel for herself. It was a tempting thought and she lifted her palm to his chest. "Maybe this will work. We'll get it out of our systems," she suggested softly. "And we won't have to wonder what it will be like anymore."

"You wonder, too?"

She hesitated before offering her honesty. "Of course."

His hand slid gently along her cheek and she raised her face to his. "I don't want you out of my system, sweetheart." His thumb tilted her chin so she couldn't look away from him. "I've wanted you since the first day I saw you. Making love with you one time isn't going to change anything."

"Will it make things worse?" She didn't like the way her voice trembled when she asked the question.

He smiled, but the corners of his mouth tilted down. "Probably, but I guess there's only one way to find out."

"I don't know about this," she began, willing her body not to react to the brush of Max's lips against hers. It didn't work. Her skin refused to cooperate, preferring instead to generously spread the exciting warmth throughout her body.

"*I* do," he murmured against her mouth. "I have all along." With that he led her upstairs.

The bedroom was dark, lighted only by the street lamp that shone across the way. Max did as he'd promised. He took his time undressing her, pulling the shirt over her head and tossing it to the floor before touching the silky skin of her breasts. Ari tried to unbutton his shirt, aching to feel his chest and rub her hands through the crinkly mat of hair. His hands circled her back and he moaned when Ari, successful finally with the buttons, explored his chest with her lips and tongue, teasing each flat male nipple before resting her cheek against his warm skin.

Max's hands slipped underneath the elastic of her shorts and his fingertips rounded the satin curve of her buttocks. "Arianna," he murmured, dipping his mouth to her earlobe. "Let's make this last." His palms pressed her against him.

Ari looked into his face and smiled. She finally felt free to touch, to explore, to do what had been building up between them since he'd hauled her down the sidewalk in Galilee. "Then I shouldn't undress you?" she asked, a teasing smile on her face.

He groaned, his fingers tightening briefly against her buttocks before sliding upward to tug at the wide waistband. He pushed the shorts down, and they fell easily past her knees to pool at Ari's ankles, where she impatiently kicked them off.

"You're beautiful," he told her.

Her face heated at the unaccustomed compliment. "You don't have to say that. I've never been, uh, model material."

"You're perfect." He sighed as he ran his palms along the dip of her waist. "I've wanted to touch you like this since the first time I saw you."

"But we were in church," she breathed, the heat between them making her weak.

"You were so gorgeous standing there in that silly, beautiful hat."

His words made her brave. She didn't know what came over her, but her shyness drifted away as his hands touched her naked body. "My turn," she answered, tugging at the snap of his jeans.

"Fair's fair," he groaned as she eased her hand inside his waistband and struggled to release the snap. "Only this might not take as long as I originally promised."

Ari wiggled her fingers against his hard abdomen. "No underwear? Very wicked of you, Captain Cole." She joked to conceal her nervousness.

"You're wearing them, remember?"

She eased the zipper down carefully but avoided touching him. Instead, suddenly unsure, she eased the pants off his hips, but felt his hard warmth against her. Max slid out of his jeans and tossed them aside. "That was fun. Now what should we do next?" There was laughter in his voice and something else, deep pleasure at having the woman he wanted with him at last.

"I don't know," Ari said. "But I wouldn't mind lying down while I think of something."

"Great idea." He shoved the bedspread onto the floor and peeled the ivory sheets away from the pillows before turning and offering Ari his hand. For a brief second she hesitated, wondering once again if he was demanding more than she was prepared to give. He seemed to understand. "No regrets," he said. "And no promises, unless you care to give them."

She shook her head slowly, admiring the gorgeous male body in front of her. He wanted her, yet was giving her a way out if she needed one. "No promises," she echoed. "Just tonight."

Max nodded. "Fair enough."

Ari walked to him as he stood beside the large expanse of mattress that awaited them. She put her hand into his, and he drew her against the warmth of his strong body. She felt his need, and a nagging worry intruded. He bent to kiss her. "Max?"

"What?"

"I don't have any birth control. I've, um, been alone for a long time."

His blue eyes warmed. "Me, too. But don't worry. I'll take care of protecting us." His lips trailed along her neck and he nibbled briefly at her earlobe, teasing the sensitive skin into shivers of need. "Ari?"

She felt as if her bones had disappeared and her muscles had given up trying to support her trembling body. "Yes?"

"Get in the bed."

8

ARI BROUGHT MAX tumbling with her onto the mattress. Their legs tangled and the heat spread, so there was no way to tell where one started and another left off. The humidity of the Rhode Island summer night clung to them as they slid against each other. Max's searching lips tasted Ari's body, relishing her sweetness and the way the nest of curls between her legs tangled in his fingers.

She touched Max for the first time, running gentle fingers along the length of him, exploring the rounded tip and feeling the satin skin beneath her fingers. And when her body cried out to be filled, Max seemed to sense it, along with his own need to be inside her. When he was, she closed around him, and they made love for long, needy moments. Ari arched beneath Max's body, feeling the climax rock through her, and he answered, his breathing ragged as his lips touched her shoulder and his teeth grazed her skin.

It was over, long after it had begun.

Neither had wanted it to stop.

"Are you certain we're never going to do this again?" he asked finally, after many silent minutes while they caught their breath and the world gently righted itself.

Delicious aftershocks rippled through Ari's body as Max moved slightly, shifting his weight so he could look at her face. "Mmm," she said, sliding her hands along the damp skin of his back. "Maybe we could work something out."

"Maybe you only want me for my body," he teased.

She closed her eyes and tried to memorize the sound of his voice. "Maybe you're right."

"Don't go to sleep," he whispered, feathering her mouth with kisses.

"Too late," she murmured, feeling herself slip over the edge of consciousness.

Max listened to her even breathing, then carefully eased himself from her. The room was still dark, and he walked over to the window. It was another clear night; the *Million* would be home tomorrow, and it was his turn next to captain the boat. Jerry loved the sea as much as he did, but Barbara was growing tired of her new husband's continued absences. All the same, the growing shipping plant was taking up more and more of Max's time. He knew he could spend the next two weeks behind a desk at Cole Products and still not get everything done he needed to.

Max looked back at the woman sleeping in his bed. He debated whether or not to cover her with the sheet, but the room was warm, despite the ocean breeze. How could he have fallen in love with a woman who didn't like boats? Didn't like the ocean and lived in some landlocked state out West? It didn't make sense, yet when he'd looked into those clear brown eyes of hers, when her hat had blown away in the wind and she'd laughed, he'd been lost. Pathetically and irrevocably lost.

Reluctantly he went into the bathroom and shut the door. He stepped into the shower stall and turned the faucets until water poured in a heated stream across his chest, hoping the noise wouldn't wake her. He wanted her to stay in his bed as long as possible. A million years would be nice.

Now all he had to do was convince Arianna.

"I HAVE TO GO," she said, waking when she felt him slide into bed beside her. She peered over his broad shoulder at the green numbers on the digital clock radio. "It's late."

"It's only eleven o'clock."

"My parents will worry."

"I'll drive you."

"I have my car."

"I'll follow you home."

Ari could tell he would only argue with everything she said. She studied those fathomless blue eyes of his and didn't want to argue. What she wanted to do was pull him down to the mattress with her, slide her body alongside his once more and make magic love together. "All right."

"Don't you look at me like that," he growled, "unless you want me to take you home in another hour." His glance swept over her naked body. "Or two."

"Don't tempt me," she said with a sigh.

"Why not?" He lowered his head, his lips grazing the sensitive skin in the hollow beneath her shoulder.

"Ouch."

"Sorry," he said, licking the red mark once. "I didn't mean to hurt you."

Ari flushed, remembering the tingling scrape of his mouth over that spot; it had coincided with the waves of pleasure between them. "You didn't."

He leaned over her, their skin touching and burning once again. He was hard against her thigh as the furry mat of hair on his chest tickled her breasts. "Do you really have to go home now?"

Ari reached for him, running her hands along his smooth back to draw him closer. "Not on your life."

Max rolled Ari onto her side, looking into her dreamy brown eyes while he took her. She slid her leg over his hip, trying to melt into him. He was big and hot and hard, and he filled her with a long, deep rhythm, one that satisfied her as nothing had before. When he tumbled her onto her back, he lifted himself onto his elbows and stopped, reaching to brush a damp lock of hair from her forehead.

"I knew it would be good, but I never imagined this," he said, his voice a caress as he looked down into her face.

He was deep inside her, thick and waiting, and Ari's voice was low. "Neither did I."

"I told you." He started the thrusting motion that would carry them over the brink. "I told you," he said again, then the silence claimed them.

IT WAS AFTER MIDNIGHT when he followed her. The road was dark and quiet, and Ari often looked into the rear-view mirror to see the comforting headlights behind her. The house was dark, too, just one light illuminating the kitchen door and part of the driveway. Ari turned off the engine and stepped out. She clutched the rolled-up beach towel under her arm and waved to Max as he turned and headed back to the Pier.

Peggy sat in the shadowy kitchen, a glass of iced tea in front of her on the table.

"Were you waiting up for me?" Ari felt guilty.

Peggy chuckled. "No. I can't take the humidity the way I used to. It's hard to sleep, so sometimes I get a cold drink in the middle of the night. It helps."

Ari sat down at the table, reluctant to leave her mother sitting alone. "The yard was clean. Did the boys help Dad clean up?"

Peggy nodded. "You did a good job. We made over three hundred dollars. Can you believe that?"

Ari chuckled. "Not really. But you had a lot of stuff to get rid of."

"A lifetime," her mother agreed wistfully. "I should have cleaned more."

"You can clean all you want in your new house."

"True. I'll like that."

They sat companionably together in the silence, listening to the crickets chirp in the backyard. Finally Ari looked at her watch. "It's almost one o'clock. Are you sure you're not waiting up for the boys?"

Peggy shook her head. "If I did that I'd never get any sleep. I figure they're old enough to take care of themselves, though I have to admit it took a lot of getting used to."

"They'll have to get their own place when you move, won't they?"

Peg nodded. "It's time." She took a swallow of tea and the ice cubes rattled loudly. "Dad said you were out with the captain. Did you have a nice time?"

Ari smiled, unable to keep the happy expression out of her eyes. "Yes, I suppose you could call it that."

"Are you in love with him?"

"I don't think I want to get into that."

Peggy eyed her daughter carefully. "All right. I'll respect your privacy, I suppose, but the captain won't take your leaving easily."

In spite of herself, Ari wanted to hear what her mother had to say. "Why not? We're both mature adults. We both agreed to the rules."

"Rules," her mother repeated, as if Ari had spoken a foreign word. She sighed. "That doesn't mean no one's going to get hurt, Arianna. And I'd hate for you to suffer again."

"I'm not going to." Her voice was firm.

"And your handsome captain? What of him?"

"I wish you'd stop calling him the captain."

Her mother raised an eyebrow. "It's a title worthy of respect."

"I call him Max."

"Are you trying to forget he's a fisherman? That he goes out to sea for a living?"

"Yes," Ari snapped and stood up. "That's exactly what I want to forget."

"You love who you love, Arianna Marie Simone. No matter what he does for a living, no matter what he looks like or where he lives."

"We're not talking about love, Mother."

"I think that's exactly what we're talking about," her mother argued. "You've made love with the captain," she whispered. "You've been in his bed, you've given your body and with it, I think, your heart. Don't take such a commitment too lightly."

"I never have," Ari whispered, turning away from her mother's piercing gaze. She turned away. "I'm going to bed now. Good night." She hurried out of the room and upstairs to the privacy of her bedroom. She stripped quickly, and put on a clean T-shirt before climbing into bed. But sleep didn't come easily. Despite the early-morning hours she'd spent working at the yard sale, despite the long, hot July day, despite hours of love-making in Max's bed, Ari couldn't sleep. She blamed it on the thick, moist air.

Blamed it on the nap she'd had in Max's bed.

Blamed it on anything but falling in love.

AIR-CONDITIONING was the only answer, Ari decided, longing for a dry Montana breeze. She couldn't sit around the house all day feeling lost. She couldn't spend her entire Sunday wondering what it would have been like to wake up in Max's arms this morning, to share coffee and breakfast and even a shower. He hadn't asked her to stay the night.

And she wouldn't have, not without making arrangements to avoid worrying her parents. Still, she longed to see Max, to look into his eyes and discover if last night had been as good between them as she remembered.

Ari broke into a sweat just thinking about it and tried to focus on her chores for the day. Shopping. Stores. Groceries. Peg had given her a list before heading to the chowder stand. Thus armed, Ari hit the Wakefield Mall first and did what she always did when she was depressed, confused, or felt as if she had a little extra money: went to the bookstore.

Thirty-seven dollars later, her bag nicely weighted with paperback fiction, Ari strolled through the rest of the small shopping area, content to poke through the sale racks and look for anything sensible, comfortable and warm to wear for the coming winter.

It was hard to concentrate. This thing with Max was just a summer romance, she told herself. Just a brief affair.

Only a one-night stand. Ari winced at the crude phrase. That wasn't her style, but she didn't know about Max. She crossed the parking lot and unlocked the car. She should be at the beach with the rest of the population of Rhode Island. But Sunday was a terrible day for going to the beach. It was better to let the city people enjoy their day off than try to find a spot on the overcrowded shore. The locals stayed home on weekends, preferring to shop or clean or putter in their yards. The city people could have the traffic and the ocean.

She wanted to drive by the seawall, see the crowds and smell the summer feeling in the air. Watch the parade of tourists along the sidewalk.

Visit the scene of the crime.

Since Ari had to deliver groceries to Peggy, she took the long way around. She drove through the Pier, got stuck in traffic only briefly, glanced longingly at the window she thought belonged to Max's bedroom, then took the winding Ocean Road into Galilee.

She parked in the corner marked Private Parking behind the fish shop, knowing Uncle Harry wouldn't have her car towed away. Otherwise he was ruthless with trespassers, and she didn't blame him. Crushed clam shells, bleached by the sun, crunched under her sandals as she stepped out and looked past the dark piers to the channel. Boats of all shapes and sizes were cruising through the harbor entrance. The air smelled of fish, the sea gulls squawked, hoping for some food, circling the boats, and people called to each other across the water.

Turning away, Ari was glad she was safely on land. She pushed open the screen door and Ruthie, sprawled in a chaise lounge, waved a greeting.

"What are you doing here?" Ari couldn't believe the very pregnant woman was content to sit in the back of a smelly fish store, swat flies and drink diet cola.

"I'm supposed to rest," Ruth admitted shyly. "But I get lonesome."

Peggy scooped chowder into a carry-out container. "And I can keep an eye on her with Coe out fishing." She winked at Ruth. "After all, I need to take care of my future granddaughters."

Ari plopped the bags of groceries onto an empty spot on the table, opened the refrigerator and helped herself to a diet soda. "You really think you're going to get a girl this time, Mom?"

"Girls," Ruthie corrected. She patted her stomach. "There are two of them in here, remember?"

"After five grandsons, though I love them all, don't get me wrong...."

Ruthie smiled at Ari. "She says that all the time."

"But we need more women in this family."

"Joey and Jimmy could get married," Ari offered.

"Lord help the women who take them on," her mother groaned. "Don't get too comfortable," Peggy warned, watching Ari pull out a metal folding chair. "I've an errand for you to run."

"Can it wait?" Ari popped the top off the can and took a long drink.

"No."

Peggy handed her a white bag. "Careful. It's hot."

Ari took it gingerly. "Why are you giving this to me?"

"The president of Cole Products ordered lunch."

"What?"

"Well," Peggy said, putting her hands on her ample hips. "You don't like me calling him the Captain."

"Why can't the president of Cole Products come get it himself?"

"He's busy. You're not." Peggy turned away and went back to the caldron on the stove. "It won't hurt you to bring the man his lunch."

"I wouldn't argue if I were you," Ruthie suggested.

"Right." Ari put the cola back into the refrigerator and left. The heat hit her with force, but the breeze from the water countered the humidity and lifted her spirits. She crossed the parking lot and walked down the broken sidewalk to the large building with Max's name on it and opened a heavy metal door marked Private Property. No Trespassing.

It was quiet, although a couple of large machines hummed at one side of the enormous room. A sign with Office spelled out in red letters pointed to a metal stairway, so Ari charged ahead, curious to see where Max spent his on-land hours.

She heard his voice before she peeked through the half-open door. Giving orders, of course. She should have known. A black telephone receiver was pressed to his ear, the dark hair was curling onto his forehead, but the absent, worried look in his blue eyes shifted immediately when he looked up and saw her. He beckoned her in and swiveled closer to the telephone, as if ready to hang up quickly.

"Fine." He listened, then somewhat impatiently added, "That's it, then." Ari waited, looking around the crowded room Max called an office. "Yeah. You, too."

"I didn't mean to interrupt big business."

He smiled, tossed the receiver onto the hook and reached for Ari. He pulled her onto his lap. "It's okay."

"Hey!" she protested. "Watch out for your lunch!"

"Is that all you brought for me?"

"Yep." She planted a quick kiss on his lips. "And it's hot, too."

"I'm going to resist making another crack," he said, his arms tightening around her. "Because you brought me something to eat."

"Just what you ordered."

His blank expression as he took the bag, letting Ari get up, tipped her off. "You didn't ask Peggy for chowder, did you?"

"No," he said. "Was I supposed to?"

"She's matchmaking," Ari explained. "She sent me here."

"I'm glad to see you. I've thought about you all morning."

"I wanted to see where you work."

"Look around all you want." He opened the bag and pulled out the carton of chowder and a plastic spoon. "You want to share this?"

"No, thanks."

"There's a soda machine downstairs. I'll get us something to drink."

"I'll come with you."

He looked surprised but let her follow him downstairs. "I'm doing paperwork, trying to catch up with May and June before I go out Tuesday morning."

Go out meant out to sea. "For how long?"

"As long as it takes."

"I hope it doesn't take very long then," she said, lifting her lips as he put his arms around her. "I'll be lonesome without you."

"I'll be back in time for the reunion."

She pulled away and looked into his eyes. "My reunion? Why?"

"Because we're going."

"No, we're not."

Max kissed her lightly before answering. "You'll have fun. It's important."

"I don't think important is the correct word to describe a fifteen-year high school reunion."

He shrugged. "You're dumping a lot of trash this summer. Maybe it's time to face the past and get rid of some more old baggage."

Ari didn't like where the conversation was headed. "Maybe it's none of your business."

"Maybe you're wrong, because I think whatever keeps you away from your family, whatever fear you have for the sea, whatever you're running away from started right here."

"And if it did, what difference does it make?"

"Talk to me, Ari."

She shook her head. "You were going to buy me a cold drink."

He ignored the hint. "You've never asked me about my family, do you know that?" He didn't wait for an answer, just went right on. "You've never asked about my parents or sisters or where I grew up, why I'm in the fishing business or how I met Jerry." He put his hands on her shoulders to keep her from turning away. "You've never asked, because you don't want to get close to me, to know me, to be part of my life—"

"*Last night* wasn't getting to know you?" She preferred to dodge the 'part of my life' complaint.

"Last night needed to happen. It was a beginning, not an ending. But it didn't exist in a vacuum."

"What do you want from me?"

"Nothing you can't give, sweetheart."

"I can only give you a few more weeks. No promises, no regrets, remember?"

He sighed, his eyes darkening as he looked down at her determined expression. "I remember." His lips brushed hers, then again. This time the pressure was strong, as if he needed to make certain she knew he meant business.

A few moments later, Ari drifted back to earth and burrowed her face into Max's striped denim shirt. His chest rumbled when he spoke. "Want to go out to dinner tonight?" She nodded, and his arms tightened around her. "Can you spend the night?"

"Possibly." Her heart turned over at the thought of having him beside her all night long.

"Try."

"I will."

He released her, led her to the bright red soda machine and fumbled through his pockets for quarters. She pushed the button for her selection and a can belched its way out. She opened it while he bought a ginger ale for himself. "Do I get a tour today?"

Max shook his head. "No. I'll never get any work done if you're around." He grinned. "You're quite a distraction."

Ari sighed and went to the door. "I'll let myself out."

"I'll pick you up at eight. Thanks for lunch."

"Thank Peg." Ari nodded and left. She walked back to her car and, unwilling to see her mother's satisfied expression, decided to go straight home. After all, she'd tried to avoid thinking about Maximilian Cole, but her feeble attempts hadn't worked. How could she justify an affair? There was no way, Ari decided, especially since she absolutely, positively refused to fall in love.

"THE SCALLOPS were delicious," Ari said in response to the waitress's question as she cleared the table.

"You're still not tired of them?" Max asked, remembering the night on Block Island. For now he was content to sit across from her in the busy Newport restaurant. The fog had rolled in, shrouding what should have been a beautiful ocean view with the familiar gray mist.

She shook her head. "Not yet."

Max couldn't take his eyes off Ari tonight. Her dark hair hung loose, curling against her shoulders, and a simple coral dress showed off her lightly tanned skin. An arrangement of matching coral beads dangled from her earlobes and brushed against her neck when she tilted her head to smile at him. "What about you?" she inquired. "Do you always order steak?"

"Almost."

"You'd like our homegrown Montana beef."

"I don't want to talk about Montana tonight."

Ari looked away. "Fine." She took a sip of wine before placing her glass on the table. "What do you want to talk about?"

"For one thing," he said, deciding it was time to set Ari straight about her ridiculous matchmaking schemes, "how many weeks did you run that damn ad in the paper?"

"A few," she said slowly, stalling.

"A few is how many exactly?"

"Six."

"Six?" He frowned at the beautiful woman who looked as if she was trying not to laugh. "I received sixty letters the first week and they're still coming in."

"I underestimated your appeal."

"You overestimated my patience."

"Have you read them all?"

He picked up his glass and absently twirled the stem. "No. Although one sent me a box of candy."

"How . . . nice. I suppose you have to thank her."

Max nodded. He didn't tell Ari the shapes of the chocolates were X-rated, or that the poem enclosed had suggested he might care to participate in a monthly sexual Olympics in Boston.

Ari wore a sheepish expression. "I didn't mean to cause you so much trouble."

"Serves you right for trying to get rid of me."

"You have a point," she admitted. "But my heart was in the right place."

Max leaned forward, wishing he could kiss her. "Speaking of right places, let's go home, shall we?"

Ari grinned at him and tossed her napkin onto the table. She took the hand Max offered and he led her around the curve of the small table until, placing one hand upon her back, he ushered her from the crowded restaurant.

Its outline marked in white lights like a spectacular Christmas decoration, the glittering Newport Bridge swept across Narragansett Bay to the Jamestown shore. Ari sat close to Max, her thigh barely touching his, as she watched the boats move beneath the bridge and the lights dot the shorelines of the islands. The fickle fog hung in the distance over the ocean, as if daring any sailors to leave the bright party in the bay and head out to sea.

"How many weeks?" Max asked suddenly in the silence.

She knew what he meant. "Three. I have to be back at school by August 28."

"That doesn't give me much time."

She didn't want to ask, but she did, anyway. "Time for what?"

"To convince you to stay."

"We've been over this before, Max."

"It bears repeating."

Ari didn't answer. She didn't want to face the future. Why couldn't he leave everything as it was? "We're a summer romance, Max."

"I think we're more than that," he said slowly.

"All right," she agreed, twisting in her seat so she could examine his strong profile in the darkness of the car. "We're the last great affair in the history of the world."

He flashed her a wry smile, then turned his attention back to the road in front of him. "Yes," he said, his voice low. "I guess we are."

The rest of the drive to Max's town house was completed in silence. They climbed the steps to his door, and Ari was afraid her heart would pound so loudly that it would drown the roar of the surf across the street. She wished he'd touch her, hold her, anything so she could rest her head against his crisp white, short-sleeved shirt and inhale the scent of his skin, but didn't know if it was wise to make the first move. He wanted so much from her—and was only setting himself up to be disappointed. He wanted everything, including her life, her freedom and her love.

The love part was easy. She'd given him everything she could, even though a summer affair went against her better judgment. Ari sighed. Max was a hard man to resist.

"Ari?" He hesitated at the door as he swung it open. "I can take you home, if you'd rather."

"Is that what you want?"

His eyes were dark, his expression guarded. "Of course not. But I'd rather not play games."

Ari suppressed a shiver as the breeze stung her bare shoulders. "Me, neither."

"You know I want you, want to make love to you."

She touched his face. "I know, and I want you, too." More than anything she'd ever wanted in her entire life.

"But?"

"I have to be home by nine. Monday's my day to peel potatoes."

"And Tuesday's my day to go to sea." Max kissed Ari's hand as she dropped it from his cheek, and she struggled to hide how much she needed him, how much she wanted him to lead her inside. Somehow she had to keep up the pretense, because if he knew she was falling in love with him he might never let her out of the state.

"Come," he said, tugging firmly on her hand. "We don't have any time to waste."

He was right. So right. So why did the admonition strike such a melancholy chord in her heart?

He sighed, his breath warm on her cheek as he pulled her against him. "I'll be good to you, Ari."

"I know," she said, her voice catching on the words. "that's the one thing I'm certain of."

He unbuttoned the back of the dress, sliding his warm, rough hands along the fine ridge of her spine and skimming along the lace waistband of her underwear. He easily unhooked her bra, then slid his searching palms to her breasts as the dress fell in a bright puddle onto the carpet. His lips teased the tip of her breast, coaxing the nipple to peak and harden under his soft ministration.

Ari reached up and put her hands onto his shoulders, and Max lifted his lips to her neck, trailing his tongue to the hollow of her throat and to the dangling corral beads.

He'd wanted to make love to her while she wore long earrings—he remembered the moment on the ferry when he'd told her his name and he'd resisted the impulse to touch the swinging pearls that brushed her silk-clad shoulder. Resisted only because he'd believed she was Jerry's troublemaker.

Well, Max decided, inhaling the light scent of flowers, she *was* trouble. But he could handle the kind of trouble she'd brought into his life.

Now he was free to touch. Free to taste whatever part of this woman's body she would share with him. Until morning.

He didn't realize he'd spoken the last words until she whispered, "What?"

"Until morning," he repeated. "We can make love until morning."

Ari pulled away from him and gazed into his eyes. Her expression looked anything but innocent. "Then why are we standing here in the living room?"

"I'm taking your clothes off, in case you haven't noticed."

"I noticed," she whispered. "Now it's my turn."

Max struggled for control while the determined woman in front of him slowly unbuttoned his shirt and eased the sleeves down his arms. When she reached for the snap on the waistband of his beige slacks, he stopped her small hand. He wanted to tell her how much he was in love with her, but stopped. He knew—from hard, painful experience—that those words would not be welcome. Instead he drew her palm to his lips and slowly kissed each soft fingertip before tugging her toward the stairs. This wasn't the time to argue.

Their remaining clothes came off quickly, and Ari sought Max's skin, longing to touch him. She took him between her hands and stroked its hard, satin length until he groaned with pleasure. Only twenty-four hours since they'd made love, and yet, Ari thought, it felt like twenty-four days or twenty-four years.

When they fell across the bed, Max covered Ari's body with kisses until she felt almost weightless with pleasure. His lips tickled her and centered between her legs as his hands held her thighs apart. He seemed to know where to touch, to sense what would please her. His fingers held her open and his tongue and lips moved to bring her to the brink of pleasure. When her body threatened to burst out of control, Max slid up to cover her.

"I want you inside me," she whispered.

His eyes crinkled at the corners and Ari traced the laugh lines etched into his face. "Whatever you want, sweetheart," he said softly, shifting slightly. He entered her with a smooth motion, filling her, burying himself in her warmth. The timeless rhythm took over and they clung to each other until the world burst around them.

Later, in the quiet darkness of the bedroom, Max held Ari close to him as she lay on her side. The mist drifted through the open window and the sound of the sea was masked by the lonely call of a nearby foghorn calling its warning to the sailors.

"Is that how they do it in Montana?"

Ari smiled against the warm skin of his shoulder. "No. It was never like that in Montana."

"There must have been someone in your life."

"Yes," she said. "A good friend, a nearby rancher."

"What happened?"

"Last year we realized we were good friends, nothing more. It was time to go in separate directions."

"I'm glad," he murmured, sliding his hand along her satiny skin. His fingertips touched her hips before making their slow journey back to her shoulder. He touched the dangling length of earring.

"I forgot to take them off," she said.

"I didn't want you to," Max told her, smiling into her dark brown eyes. "Since Jerry's wedding I've discovered I have an earring fetish."

Ari struggled to sit up and leaned over Max's chest so she could see him better. "I've never heard of that."

He grinned. "Maybe I'm unique."

"I'm sure of it," she agreed. "For more than one reason. Lift your head," she ordered, reaching for a fluffy white pillow. She tucked it behind his head.

"What are you doing?" he asked. Despite his amusement, he felt himself harden again.

Ari slid her body over his and kissed his lips. "If you don't have any objections, I thought I'd show you how it's done out West."

9

"HERE," Max said, handing Ari a steaming mug. "Don't worry. You don't have to talk."

"Thanks." Ari smiled at him, then turned her attention to the thick mug cradled in her hand. She sat wrapped in a blanket in a comfortably padded lounge chair on Max's balcony. The early-morning sun struggled to burn off the remainder of last night's fog, and Ari silently cheered its efforts.

Max left the balcony and she heard him banging pots and pans in the kitchen. She assumed he was busy making himself one of the horrendously huge breakfasts of which he was so fond. She smelled bacon and knew she'd guessed right. In a minute he opened the door and stuck his head out. "Ari, do you want bacon and eggs? Just shake your head yes or no."

"I'm not that bad," she protested, turning to see him. He looked incredibly handsome. His hair was still damp from the shower, and he wore the familiar denim jeans and Nebraska T-shirt. He also looked very hungry.

"Yes, you are."

"No to breakfast, then. I'll have an early lunch at work."

He nodded and closed the door, leaving her to the peace and quiet of the balcony and the Narragansett morning. She watched cars cruise along the road below, watched the traffic light change colors, saw several determined joggers pound the sidewalk and three people walking their dogs. Ari leaned back, finished the rest of her coffee and lazily decided whether or not to get up and fetch herself another cup.

It was quiet in the kitchen now. *You've never asked me about my family... because you don't want to get close, to be part of my life.* Had Max been fair when he'd said that yesterday? Ari tried to think objectively and realized she knew the man liked breakfast, enjoyed his steak rare, polluted his coffee with cream and drove a truck. He successfully ran Cole Products, owned several fishing boats and lived within sight of the ocean.

Always the ocean.

He'd played high school football and was great in bed. Generous, caring, determined and persistent.

Also uncompromising and passionate.

Ari sighed. She knew the qualities of the present-day Maximilian Cole, but nothing of what had made him the man he was today or of the forces that had shaped his life.

Very heavy thinking. Much too heavy for a summer romance.

She heard the door open again and Max's footsteps on the wooden deck.

"Here," he said kindly, holding out the coffeepot. "I forgot you usually need nine or ten cups."

"Three," she corrected, handing him the mug. "Three cups guarantees a very nice person."

"You were a very nice person last night." He poured the hot liquid without spilling and carefully handed the cup back to her.

"So were you."

"Two nights in a row," he said. "It could become a habit."

"It could," she agreed, loving the way his eyes crinkled at the corners. Why wasn't he within touching distance? "But you're going out on the *Million* tomorrow, aren't you?"

He nodded. "Yeah. Today's going to be busy."

"Maybe you'd better get started."

"Maybe I'd better take you back to bed."

Ari pretended to think it over. She looked at her watch, set down the coffee and grinned at Max. "Do you have the time?"

"I'll make it quick."

She laughed. "You'd better not."

"I'll make it last, then. You won't have the energy to pick up a paring knife."

"That's okay," Ari said, unwrapping herself from the blanket so she could stand up. Max's T-shirt hung to her knees. The boards were cool to her bare feet, although the sun was beginning to win its battle with the fog. "I'll risk it."

ARI SWAM every evening at six. Wore the same bathing suit, parked in the same corner of the lot, said the same prayers to the water lapping around her body. *Keep him safe. Please, keep him safe.* More of an appeal than a threat, granted, but Ari couldn't stop the words from running through her head every time she looked to the horizon, wondering where Max was and if he was all right.

She hated it, hated the worry and the nauseous feeling in the pit of her stomach. Hated waking up uneasy and going to bed at night listening to the weather sta-

tion on the radio. Hated herself for acting like such a
cowardly fool.

"YOU SHOULD GO. You'll have fun."

"You sound like a broken record," Ari said, determined to ignore her mother's advice. Peg had been
saying the same thing for the last nine hundred and
eighty-seven potatoes. Or five days, whichever way a
person preferred to judge the time.

But Peggy persisted. "They're not going to make
records anymore. I heard that on TV. Isn't that a
shame?"

"You watch too much TV."

"What am I supposed to do with all those old al-
bums you kids left in the closets?"

"I sold them at the yard sale, so don't give it another
thought."

"I don't know what I would have done this summer
if it hadn't been for you. I still don't know how I'm going
to move all of our belongings into that little house in
town."

"I thought you liked the new house."

"I do. It's such a lot of work, though."

Ari frowned at the potato in her hand. "When's Russ
buying the house?"

"In the fall. Your father says the boys will be a big help
when the time comes to move. I'll believe it when I see
it." Ari had her doubts, too, but kept silent. She'd finish cleaning out what she could, but there'd be nothing
she could do from Bozeman. Peggy sighed. "I wish you
weren't so far away."

Ari winked at Ruth. "You say that every day."

"I worry about you. You're a good girl, Ari, but
sometimes you don't . . ."

Ari glared at her mother making her stop whatever she was going to say. "Don't *what?*"

Peggy looked pointedly at the mangled potato in her daughter's hand. "Don't know how to peel a potato, of course."

"Of course." Ari tossed it onto the table. "I'm sick of potatoes."

"So? You're not forced to be here. Go home and get ready to go out tonight."

Ari thought of struggling to remember the names of classmates she hadn't seen in fifteen years. "I don't want to."

Ruthie walked slowly to the refrigerator. "You can go to the movies with me and Coe, if you want."

"No, thanks. You two need to be alone while you still have the chance."

"The babies aren't due for another six weeks." Ruth rubbed her back. "Though sometimes I wonder if they're anxious to make their entrance."

Concern for her daughter-in-law made Peggy frown. "You should be home resting."

"I can rest here. Besides, I hate being home alone. Coe's out with Kevin, but they should be hauling back any day now. He was hoping to get on that construction crew, building that new bank, so he'd be home at night."

Ari remembered when her older brother had built the world's most elaborate tree house. "He always was happier with a hammer and nails."

"Some men aren't cut out for the sea," Peggy said. "No harm in that."

"And some don't think they should do anything else," Ari muttered.

"There's no changin' them, you know." Peggy frowned a warning at her only daughter. "The pain comes from living without them."

"Eddie's gone," Ari said softly, standing up to look past the screen door to the docks. "That was pain, Mom."

"I'll not be arguing with that," Peg answered, her voice soft with sympathy. "But it's time you dealt with it and put it to rest."

"I thought I had."

"No," Peggy declared, shaking her head as she patted Ari's shoulder. "Don't you understand, honey? You've only been running away from it."

Later, Ari stood alone in her bedroom and heard her mother's words echoing in her head, *running away from it*. Was that what she was doing?

She stripped off her work clothes and grabbed her robe. The party started in an hour. Running away, huh? There was only one way to find out.

IT WAS a pretty normal-looking group, although some members of the class of '75 looked slightly uncomfortable in the noisy cocktail lounge of the popular 'Gansett Club. An unofficial gathering, there were no name tags, no balloons or class rosters. A few people wandered around with yearbooks under their arms, and Ari wished she'd brought hers. Not for sentiment, but because it might make it easier to identify the unfamiliar grown-ups wandering through the bar with drinks in their hands.

"Hey, Simone!" a deep voice called as Ari threaded her way through the crowd. She'd spent the last half hour politely smiling at people who politely smiled back, occasionally running into childhood friends—the kind of people who remembered when she used to eat the dirt in the sandbox.

A cheerful-looking man held out his hand. "Arianna? Remember me?"

"Johnny Kenyon. Sure." Ari was so thrilled with herself for actually recognizing someone that she forgot to be nervous. Besides, how could an English professor let a mere couple of hours at a high school reunion turn her into a total idiot? Get a grip, Simone.

"You look great. You haven't changed a bit."

"Neither have you," she fibbed.

"What are you doing now?"

"I teach at Montana State."

He whistled. "You don't look like a professor," Johnny said. "And you're married with kids, I suppose?"

Ari shook her head. "Not yet." *Not yet?* Okay, I'm an optimist. Somewhere out West there was another eligible farmer, one with no desire to catch fish.

"I see your brothers around town once in a while."

"They all still live in Narragansett!" Ari shouted over the pounding Rolling Stones song blasting from a nearby speaker. Someone had turned the volume to High.

"Nice seeing you again!" He shrugged at the loudness of the music and moved away.

Well, now what? When in doubt a woman could head for the ladies' room or climb onto a bar stool and flirt with the bartender, only in this case the bartender looked about thirteen years old and was way too busy to have time to flirt with a Montana spinster.

The class of '75 enjoyed partying, no doubt about it.

"You could have waited for me," a rough voice said into her ear.

Ari turned around to see Max, handsome in a blue shirt that matched his eyes, his cheekbones tinged with sunburn and his strong brown arms folded across his chest. "It wasn't necessary," she said.

"No?"

She shook her head for added emphasis. "Look," she stated, hoping he could hear her over the music. "I had a life before I went to bed with you. I'm thirty-two years old and I live by myself and I make my own decisions and—"

He swore, grabbed her arm and hustled her through the crowd to the veranda, not stopping until they had stepped down to the minuscule, rocky beachfront. Finally he let her go and inhaled the fresh smell of the sea. "I missed you. It's been a long—but profitable—four days."

"What are you trying to prove?" The rock and roll was a muffled bass guitar beat in the background, and the low tide's odor drifted through Ari's nostrils.

"That was supposed to be my next question," he snapped back. "You had a real case against going to this reunion. What made you change your mind?"

"I'll get into it with you later," Ari responded, suddenly tired. She had missed him so dreadfully, hated every minute that he was out to sea. Now he stood in front of her, strong and gorgeous and . . . *alive*. And all she could do was pick a fight with him because he was there in front of her, when she'd been so angry while he was far away. "You can save the caveman technique for someone else."

"I know how old you are and I'm fully aware of the fact that you have your own life—you keep reminding me of it often enough—but you could at least have saved me the effort of going to your house."

"I didn't know you were back," Ari lied. She'd seen the *Million* coming through the channel when she'd left the fish store.

"You didn't want me involved."

"If you honestly believed that, then why are you here right now?"

He shrugged. "Maybe I'm a fool."

Ari knew she should agree, but felt guilty about picking a fight with him. She could have left a message for him instead of rushing off by herself. She hadn't wanted him involved, though, hadn't wanted him to know too much about her. It was as if the knowledge would give him power. Power to hurt.

Power to heal.

"Look," she said, putting her hand upon his strong brown arm—to keep him from moving away into the sea? "Maybe this isn't going to work. You're awfully possessive and I'm not used to being treated that way."

"You'd better get used to it," he growled, his eyes glinting as he looked down at her. "Damned used to it."

Uncompromising idiot. She took her hand away. "This is my reunion and—"

"I thought you needed some company."

"Not really." She didn't want to give him the satisfaction of knowing he was right. "I've been here an hour, and I've had a good time."

"You're telling me to get lost."

Ari shrugged, unable to stop herself. All she wanted to do was get out of Rhode Island.

"Fine." Without another word, Max swiveled, walked up the rough wooden steps and across the porch to disappear inside the inn, leaving Ari standing in the fading sunlight. She sighed, stuck her hands into the pockets of her bright coral sundress and slowly climbed the steps in her turn. But instead of following Max inside, she walked around the west end of the veranda toward the parking lot.

Max ordered a double scotch on the rocks and leaned against the bar. He hadn't minded crashing the party— after all, he probably knew more people here than Arianna. He paid for his drink and took a swallow as the music suddenly stopped and a microphone squawked. An excited voice announced, "Class of '75!"

There was a smattering of applause and a couple of rowdy cheers. One person booed. Max would have smiled if he'd been in the mood. He couldn't see who was talking, because the crowd by the bar hid his view, but he didn't care.

He'd gone to a hell of a lot of trouble to make it here tonight, and Ari hadn't even appreciated the effort. He'd sip his scotch and head for home. There would be no woman in his bed tonight—no warm, willing, loving Arianna to welcome the sailor home from the sea. He must have been crazy to think that was what would happen.

"Can I have your attention?" The announcer didn't wait for an answer. "I have a couple of things to talk to you about tonight, but first of all, let's have a round of applause for the man who put all of this together, the illustrious president of the class of '75—Barney Charpentier!" Barney stood up and took a bow, then the self-appointed announcer continued. "I have a number of messages to read, some letters we received from classmates who couldn't make tonight's gathering." He read several warm letters from faraway friends, then went on to ask for a moment of silence for those who had died—one couple in a traffic accident, another person from cancer, and a certain Eddie Barton, who'd been swept overboard from his fishing boat.

Max straightened, holding his glass carefully so no sound would interrupt the silence. *Swept overboard from his fishing boat?* He waited for a few minutes until the rest of the announcements were over, the music blasting again before he started searching the crowd for Ari. When he didn't see her, Max stationed himself by the entrance to the women's bathroom for twenty minutes. He finally drifted away to talk to a group of men who worked in Galilee. He was looking for answers, and if Ari wouldn't talk to him, he'd find someone who would give him some.

"YOU SNEAKED OUT," he said when Ari opened the kitchen door.

"I didn't sneak anywhere," she answered mildly. "I simply got into my car and drove away. In plain sight of everyone."

"I have dinner waiting in the truck," Max told her, unwilling to enter the Simone house. He wanted an uninterrupted conversation with Ari, and the Simones' place wasn't where he wanted to have it. "Come back to my place with me and we'll eat." When Ari hesitated, Max added, "I'm guessing you haven't had dinner."

"No."

"Then what's the problem?"

"There isn't one." Ari held the door open wider. "Come on in while I write a note. The boys are off partying and Mom and Dad are babysitting for Russ while he and Karen are shopping for carpet. They think I'm still at the reunion."

"You missed the announcements," Max said, watching as she rifled through a drawer and found a pencil. "Or did you?"

The blank expression on her face told him she'd left before the class president's speech. "So?"

He watched her carefully. "Eddie Barton drowned. We had a moment of silence for him and some other people who died." She stood very still, her hair hiding her profile as she bent to write on the pad of paper on the table. "But I'll bet you already knew about Eddie, didn't you?"

"Yes," she said, her voice soft. "I already knew about Eddie."

Max stepped closer. He wanted to touch her but didn't know if she'd even notice. "Are you going to tell me about it?"

She looked up at him, her eyes dry. "I was in love with Eddie Barton all through high school. Blond, brown-eyed Eddie. His hair would turn white in the summertime, lighter than his eyebrows, as if nature had played a trick on him. He was my best friend in grade school, my tormentor in junior high and my boyfriend in high school."

"And?"

"I wasn't a cheerleader or a prom queen or even a brain, but I was Eddie Barton's girl and planned to be Eddie Barton's wife as soon as I could talk my parents into letting us get married." She paused to brush the hair back from her face, then stared at Max. "You can't possibly want to hear any of this," she said. "Your dinner's getting cold."

"Come home with me now," Max offered, taking her hand. He didn't have to be a genius to figure out the rest of the story, and Ari's pallor worried him. He kept a firm grip on her cold hand. He didn't release her, even when she grabbed her purse, turned off the kitchen light and secured the lock on the back door. He didn't relax until, minutes later, they crossed the threshold of his home.

Ari, carrying the pizza box, started to head toward the kitchen, but Max caught her by the shoulder. "Let's eat upstairs," he suggested.

"In bed?"

"Why not?" She didn't answer, so Max lightly squeezed her shoulder before releasing her. "I'll grab some sodas. Go on up."

When he entered his bedroom a few minutes later, Ari sat cross-legged on the bed. She'd changed since the reunion, he noticed for the first time. Her long-sleeved blue shirt had Big Sky Country printed in yellow letters across the chest, and her jeans were pale blue, almost white. She'd kicked her sandals off and left them on the carpet.

Max set the six-pack of diet cola on the bed beside her and tossed a stack of paper plates beside the pizza. Ari took the roll of paper towels from under his arm and unrolled a couple of feet. "What if we spill on this bedspread?"

Max shrugged. "We wash it. Eating pizza in bed is one of life's luxuries."

Ari had already lifted the lid of the box and scooped a piece onto a paper plate. She handed it to Max. "Here. Have a good time." She served herself, licking the sticky cheese from her fingers. "Good, it's still warm."

He waited until she'd eaten two pieces and opened a can of soda. He wanted to see her back to normal before he questioned her again. She might think he was through probing, but he wasn't. Instead he waited. "You left the 'Gansett in a hurry."

"Not really. I stayed as long as I wanted to and then I left."

"Correction, ran away."

She frowned at him and sat very still. "I don't think that's fair."

He nodded. "All right. Tell me about how you were going to get married."

"It isn't very interesting."

"To me it is."

She looked away and wiped her hands with the towel. "My parents insisted I go to college, so I worked part-time as a secretary and put myself through school. Eddie jumped on his uncle's trawler and went to sea. Five years later we were still together and planning a wedding. Meanwhile Eddie and his cousins bought their own boat and were starting to make pretty good money."

Max waited, knowing the rest wasn't going to be easy to hear. "And?"

"It's the same old story, isn't it, Max?" Her smile didn't meet her eyes. "There was a bad storm. You can fill in the rest."

"And you left Rhode Island."

She shook her head. "Not right away. It took me two more years to get my master's degree, then I applied for jobs as far away from Rhode Island as I could get."

"Did leaving really help?"

Her eyes were shiny with unshed tears as she looked across the bed at him. "It sure as hell did."

"No one ever dies in Montana?"

"Not at sea." She was daring him to argue with her and he damn well wanted to.

"No one falls off mountains or gets eaten by bears or kicked in the head by their horse?"

"I can deal with avalanches and car accidents."

"How do you know?"

She was silent. "I don't want to continue this," she said finally, gathering up the trash from the bed.

"People die, Ari."

"I recognize that fact."

"Stop with the garbage," he ordered, reaching to clasp her wrist. "You can't get up and run every time this comes up."

She glared at him. "It's worked so far."

"Let it go, hon," he begged. "There's a whole world in front of us. Don't screw it up."

Ari shook her head. "There's just you and me and the summer. The summer that's almost over."

"That's what you always say. You really think it's going to be over because you drive off into the sunset?"

"You think you have a choice?"

"Don't you?" He watched her struggle to hide her feelings, watched her silently wonder what to say. It was as if she thought she could pack up all her feelings and fold them into a suitcase. A suitcase to be stored on the top shelf of her closet.

Ari tugged her arm free of Max's grip and tenderly reached over to stroke his cheek. "I don't know, Max. I just don't know."

"Maybe you don't, sweetheart," he said, gently folding her into his arms. *But I do.*

THE TEARS slipped out under her eyelashes, hot and steady, a surprising trickle into her hair. Max moved over her, his hard body joined with hers, seemingly oblivious to the turmoil of her emotions. The swirling pain of her memories mixed with the pleasure Max gave her, and Ari bit her lip to keep from crying out. It was so good she didn't want it to stop, yet her heart ached so hard that she didn't know how she could stand another second of the pain.

The tremors in her body took her by surprise, and Max thrust deep and hard, prolonging her pleasure. Ari cried out and moments later Max answered her, his lips tasting the salty tears on her skin as he held her close.

"It's going to be all right," he murmured. Ari didn't answer. Her throat was clogged with tears; she didn't want to embarrass herself by bursting into noisy sobs, which she knew she was sure to do if she tried to speak. He rolled them onto their sides and tucked Ari's head into the crook of his arm. She breathed in the wonderful smell of his skin and wished she could stay in his arms forever. Exhausted, she closed her eyes and wept silently until she fell asleep.

"CAN YOU TALK NOW?"

"Sure." Ari nodded, having silently consumed half a pot of coffee before eight o'clock. The covers lay tangled around her, and she'd propped herself on a couple of Max's enormous bed pillows. She pulled her attention away from the intriguing stack of envelopes and letters addressed to Max that lay in a messy pile on the floor beside the bed. Ari was surprised she hadn't stepped on them last night.

Max frowned when he saw her look away. "Go ahead," he told her. "Look through them. After all, you wrote the ad."

Ari shook her head. Just the fact that they were in his bedroom annoyed the hell out of her. Reading them would probably tip her over the edge. "No, thanks."

He bent and picked a blue-edged letter from the top of the pile. "Here's one." He looked down at the print and then back to Ari. "She's looking for an adventurous companion, lives on Block Island and likes to race sailboats."

"Sounds perfect." Ari wasn't going to ask Max why the replies to the ad were in his bedroom or why so many of the envelopes had been opened. He must have read some, must have been interested.

He nodded toward the pile of paper. "Quite a haul, isn't it?"

"Yes," she snapped, still annoyed. The whole thing, designed to keep Max's attentions elsewhere, had been her idea in the first place. She was an idiot.

"Don't you want to read through them, pick out the perfect woman for me?" He smiled when she glared at him, then knelt on the bed and dropped the unread letter onto the sheet. "Give yourself credit, sweetheart. You wrote one hell of an ad."

"I simply listed your . . . needs," she protested, moving her feet so he wouldn't crunch them with his weight.

"But you described me." He chuckled. "Made me sound like a cross between Kevin Costner and Errol Flynn."

"Who's Kevin Costner?" she teased, smiling into Max's dark eyes. The man had a point, though. She'd written an irresistible description of a man whose charms she couldn't withstand. "You going to call the lady sailboat racer?"

"Uh-uh," he said, drawing closer. "Opposites attract." The paper crunched as Max leaned forward and kissed her, his lips warm and demanding. Ari reached up and held his face, enjoying the way his morning whiskers scraped against the palms of her hands. When he lifted his head, he stared at her for a long moment. "Are you okay?"

"Yes." Ari felt pounds lighter, as if last night's tears had dissolved the weight around her heart. She hadn't even known it was there to begin with. The reunion hadn't killed her, and telling Max about Eddie hadn't done her in, either. Aside from having itchy eyes to remind her of her tears, she'd suffered no repercussions from last night. First chance she got, though, she was going to shove those letters under the bed. Out of sight, out of mind. "I feel . . . much better."

"Good." Max moved away from the bed and turned to the window. He shoved his hands into the pockets of his jeans and faced the sound.

"What about you?"

He turned back to her. "I've been in love with you since the very first day I met you. Did you know that?"

He returned his attention to the window and didn't see her wince. "I . . . I love you, too, Max," she answered softly, surprising herself with the words. The ceiling didn't fall, lightning didn't strike and the world didn't come to an end because she admitted she'd fallen in love with Maximilian Cole.

He swiveled from the window and stood at the foot of the bed. His face looked hard. "Then do something about it."

"There's nothing—"

"Yes," he interrupted. "There is. Stay in Rhode Island, Ari. We'll work it out."

"How? Will you stop fishing? Stop going out to sea?"

Silence met her question. His ocean-blue gaze held hers for a long moment. "It's my life. My work."

"You have the plant."

"I can't spend the rest of my life behind a desk."

"And I can't spend the rest of *my* life wondering if you're going to come home around the breakwater safe and sound."

He held out his hands to her, begging for her understanding. "I don't know how to fight this, sweetheart. You can't think I'm going to die every time I go out?"

The phone rang, harsh in the silence. Neither one moved to answer it, until Ari dropped her eyes from Max's gaze. He went to the other side of the bed and lifted the receiver to his ear. "Hello." Ari watched his lips turn down. "When?" His sharp tone surprised her. He looked at Ari and she knew the call concerned her. "Yeah, she's here. Sure."

"What?" Her heart was suddenly squeezed with tension.

He hung up the phone. "Ruthie's in labor, but it's not going well and Peg needs your help."

"Coe's not due in until tomorrow."

Max nodded. "They've got him on the radio, but it'll be a while before he can get here to be any help."

Ari jumped out of bed, kicked the letters out of her way, and looked for her clothes. "What do you mean— it's not going well?"

"They're premature, hon. That's all your mother said."

"Where are they? South County Hospital?"

He nodded. "For now."

"What does that mean?"

"I think we'd better get over there and find out."

"We?"

Max smiled and touched her cheek. "Haven't you figured that part out yet?"

10

THE GRANDDAUGHTERS Peggy and Rusty had been waiting for were born at eleven thirty-two Sunday morning. Their father and Uncle Kevin were still forty miles away, with three-quarters of a load on and several thousand pounds of fish left to sort. Since Aunt Karen wanted to be at the hospital, Uncle Russ was home with the children. He'd been anxiously waiting the birth of the babies, so he could haul his lobster traps before any overcurious tourists could ruin the day's profits. Linda had left the two toddlers with a neighbor, remembering how she'd felt when Kevin had been at sea when their youngest was born eighteen months ago. The paternal grandfather sent Joey and Jimmy home and continued to pace the hospital floor with Captain Cole. Ruthie was doing fine, but the babies were tiny, not quite four pounds each.

"I've caught lobsters far bigger than that, especially in the old days," Rusty told Max as they stood together near the doorway of the waiting room.

"Georges Bank," Max said, hoping he could keep the man's worries from his new grandchildren for a few minutes.

"Four-foot cod and forty-pound lobsters." Rusty grinned. "Remember those days, son?"

Max nodded. "Now it's a hundred and thirty miles out, and even with the net sensors I added this year, I still don't know if I'm going to haul enough back to pay the mortgage on the boat."

Rusty shook his head. "The money's not there like it used to be, son. It's not in catchin' like it used to be. My boys won't listen to me—guess it's in their blood—but you, now you're smarter."

Max shrugged. "I'm just like anyone else."

"But you've got your father's plant, and you've managed to pick up some of the foreign business. Shipping overseas, now that's where the future is."

"I'm working on it," Max admitted. He and Jerry were trying to decide who would go to Japan in the fall for an overdue business trip.

"And what about my daughter?"

"I'm working on that, too, sir." He added the sir as a genuine gesture of respect.

"You going to marry her? I don't like her spending the night with you, I'll be honest, though Ari's old enough to know her own mind . . . but I want her treated respectfully."

Max looked across the waiting room at Ari. She'd barely had time to comb her hair and yet she looked beautiful. Except for the shirt, which reminded him unpleasantly of Montana. "I'd marry her, if she'd have me."

"Hmph." Max couldn't tell if Ari's father was smiling or frowning. The red beard hid his expression. "She's a damned independent woman."

"Yes, sir."

"Thinks she knows her own mind."

"I admire that, but sometimes she drives me crazy."

Rusty shook his head. "You can't chain her to the deck, son. If she wants you it had better be her own idea."

"She'll want me," Max said, his voice firm as he watched Ari move toward them. But he knew he was lying. He didn't know any such thing.

"The doctor said we can see Ruth as soon as she comes out of the anesthesia. It was a pretty routine C-section."

"Routine?" Rusty repeated incredulously.

Ari shrugged. "You know doctors. They stay calm."

"And the little girls?"

"Are improving. The pediatrician, Dr. Bord-Something, will transfer them up to the city as soon as they're stabilized. They're tiny but strong."

"Good Simone stock," Rusty said, clearly trying to reassure himself.

Ari squeezed his arm. "That's right, Dad."

"I'm going to head to the plant and see if I can get the *Peggy Lou* on the radio," Max offered. "Coe must be going crazy right about now."

"We don't know their names," Ari pointed out. "Maybe their father will have some ideas."

"Their father is probably in shock," Rusty commented, shaking Max's hand. "See if you can calm him down."

"I'll try." Max drew Ari away down the corridor toward the exit. "Tell me the truth," he said, when they stood outside on the sidewalk. Heat blasted from the parking lot. "How are the babies?"

"It looks good. I guess twins usually come early, so nobody was too surprised. The doctor said they're pretty well developed, but will need some watching."

Max sighed. "Good." He looked back at the building. "I hate hospitals."

"Thanks for keeping Dad company. We're pitifully short of male support."

He looked at her worried expression and said, "Hey, it's going to be okay."

"I know." Ari's voice was shaky. "The girls are going up to a hospital in Providence and Ruth will be able to come home with us in a couple of days. Mom's going to spoil her and take care of her—she doesn't have any other family."

"Family's important."

"So I've heard. Where is yours?"

"It's ninety degrees and we're standing in a parking lot when you finally ask me a personal question? Lady, your timing couldn't be worse."

Ari shrugged, smiling up at him. "Are you cranky because you didn't get much sleep?"

"No breakfast, remember? Want to get lunch now?"

"No, thanks. I'll stay here and keep Dad company." She stood on tiptoe and kissed Max goodbye. "Let me know if you get in touch with Coe."

He nodded. "I'm going right to the plant."

"I'll be manning the chowder stand later. I don't think Mom's in any condition to work today. See you later."

"Yeah," he said, kissing her once more. "We have a lot to talk about."

No, we don't was what she wanted to say, but Ari watched Max walk across the parking lot, get into his truck and drive away before she climbed the steps to the hospital entrance. She'd see Max later, but didn't plan to talk to him about staying in Rhode Island and living with him. She'd have to give up her job, and she was up for tenure this year. It wasn't the greatest job in the world, and Montana had a Canadian wind that could freeze you on the spot in January, but still...it was home and she loved it.

She loved the mountains, the people, the prairie and the steak dinners at the Three Bears Café. She liked the poker games on Friday nights and the country and western bar just east of town that played live music on Saturday nights. She liked grading papers on Sundays while snow bombarded the town. She liked driving her Western pals crazy by rooting for the New England Patriots during football season. She loved her apartment, although she'd saved enough for a down payment on a small house and looked forward to house-shopping this fall. Bozeman was, well, home.

Ari tried to imagine Max in Montana, but the picture refused to appear. She could picture Max in her cozy double bed, but that was about it. The phrase "like a fish out of water" would fit Captain Maximilian Cole if he ever tried to put down roots on the solid Montana plains.

We'll work it out, he'd said. Sure, Ari knew how. If *she* gave up everything—her job, her apartment, her privacy. If she moved back to Rhode Island and lost her independence and her peace of mind. If she spent the rest of her life worrying about a man who could be swept overboard and whose body might never be found.

And for what? For love? It hadn't worked last time. She'd been left with a degree, a wedding dress and an empty future.

For a town house at the Pier? She could sit on that balcony and watch the ocean—alone—every summer morning. And every night. Big thrill.

For brown-eyed, dark-haired babies? Ari banished the vision before it became too tempting. She could have all the babies she wanted if she married someone out West.

Besides, Max hadn't mentioned marriage.

The hospital door slid open and Ari went inside. Her father waved to her from across the hall.

"Honey?"

Ari hurried over to him. "What?"

Rusty grinned and grabbed his daughter in a bear hug. "Ruthie's awake and feeling good. Said she knew all along she'd have girls."

Ari smiled. "Probably because she wouldn't dare disappoint Mom."

"Buy an old man a cup of coffee, would you?" He wiped tears of relief from the corners of his eyes. "I'm feeling a mite overwhelmed."

THE NEXT WEEK swept by, with Ari filling in for Peggy at the fish shop, and sometimes driving Ruthie to the city to see her tiny children. Amy Linette, named after Ruthie's mother, and Ann Margaret, after Peggy, were growing, adding ounces to their weight. Once they reached the five-pound mark they would come home.

In between the chowder stand, trips to the hospital and feeding whoever showed up at dinnertime, Ari managed to clean the upstairs bedrooms and pack boxes of possessions that would go into storage until Peggy decided if she wanted—or needed—them in the new house. Ari had seen the new home and thought it would be perfect for her parents, if they'd only get rid of more stuff. She was tempted to have another yard sale, but there wasn't enough time. She had a lot to do before she flew home, and was glad Max had left her alone to do it.

Thursday afternoon Ari stuck masking tape onto the things she thought could be given away. With five children living nearby, someone should be able to use some extra furniture, especially since Jim and Joey had found a house to rent. Finished with that, she went downstairs to the kitchen to see if anyone was around for dinner.

"Go! Get out of here!" Peggy waved at Ari, trying to shoo her into the living room. "You've done enough this summer. If we work you too much you'll never come back."

Ari laughed. "I liked it." It was the truth—she had liked feeling like part of the family again. Liked feeling that she mattered, that somehow she was connected. She'd even envied Ruth—not just for her exquisite little daughters, but for the protective circle the Simones created with their love and caring for one another. She might even miss it when she left.

"Go do something else," her mother ordered. "It's too hot to cook. If you want to go out for sandwiches with us, let me know."

"Did you get Ruthie settled?"

Peggy nodded. "I bought groceries so she won't have to fight the summer people in town. Her friends have brought over casseroles, too, and Coe said the girls can come home next week."

"They're beautiful," Ari observed.

"I can't wait to get my hands on them," Peggy told her, "but your father says I can't be a nuisance and should wait till I'm asked."

"You'll be asked." Ari wondered how a new mother managed with one baby. She certainly couldn't figure out how anyone could take care of two at the same time.

"You go call the captain. Have him take you somewhere nice for dinner."

Somewhere nice would mean his house. Somewhere nicer would be in his bed. She hadn't wanted to think about how much she'd missed him, but couldn't help grinning like an idiot at the thought of seeing him. "I think that's a great idea, Mother. I'm going to do just that."

There was no answer when she dialed his number, so she called the plant. His voice was gruff. "Cole Products."

"Hi."

"Ari?"

"Who else?"

"I've been holed up in this office all week, thinking about you and wondering when I could haul you out of the house."

"Tonight okay?" she inquired, unwilling to add more with her mother listening three feet away.

"How soon?"

"I'll pick up something for dinner and see you in an hour." She hung up the phone to face her mother's amused expression.

Peggy tried in vain to hide her grin. "Guess I won't leave the porch light on tonight?"

"Aren't you supposed to be shocked?" Ari teased, wondering if there was any hot water left for a shower. She pulled the elastic from her hair and let it fall to her shoulders.

"Those brothers of yours wore me out. There couldn't be another shock left in me." She patted her daughter's cheek. "I'd give you advice but you don't want any, so go—go be with Max while you can."

SHE WAS WRAPPED in Max's embrace seconds after he opened the door. "You're squishing the sandwiches," she said finally, reluctant to pull away from his bare chest. He smelled like soap, and his warm skin against her cheek made her want to pull him down to the carpet.

"I thought that was you."

She smiled up at him. "Thanks a lot."

"Well, it's been so long...."

"Four days?"

Max shrugged and released her. "Seems longer, sweetheart."

A stab of pain shot through her when she thought of leaving in two weeks. How could she have let herself fall in love this summer? Ari tried to smile. "Are you hungry?"

His eyes crinkled at the corners in the way she loved. "I can wait."

She held up the bag containing Italian submarine sandwiches. "What about these?"

Max slipped one finger under the strap of her blue tank top and edged it off her shoulder. "No bra? I like that."

"The sandwiches, Max?"

"We'll take them upstairs and eat them later. How come you've never worn this denim miniskirt before?"

"I found it when I was cleaning out my closet."

"I like it," he murmured. His fingers trailed past her breasts to her waist, then unfastened the snap at the waistband and slowly unzipped the fly.

"I thought you wanted to go upstairs."

"Not anymore," Max said, slipping the material past her hips and letting it drop to the floor.

"Well?" Ari didn't feel the least bit self-conscious standing half-naked in the foyer. She slipped off her sandals and kicked them aside while she waited for Max's reaction.

"You wore them."

She tossed the bag of food onto a nearby chair, before turning to smile. "Didn't you say you wanted to take them off?"

"More than anything else in the world." His words were low as his hands cupped her bare waist and pulled her to him. Minutes later the peach silk panties slithered to the carpet.

Max's lips were warm against her neck. "Think we can make it to the bed?"

"We could try." Ari tossed her tank top aside before Max swung her into his arms.

"I've always wanted to carry a naked woman upstairs to my bed," he whispered, taking a deep breath. Ari curled her hands around his neck.

"I should have put that in the ad," she murmured.

"That damn ad," Max cursed, edging sideways through the bedroom doorway, "has made me the laughingstock of the post office."

Ari nestled her face in the furry mat on his chest. "Put me down and I'll make it up to you." He tossed her onto the unmade bed and followed her down. Sunlight, muted by the window shades, gave a faint yellow glow to the white sheets. "No fair," she said, reaching for him. "You're still wearing jeans."

"I can fix that," he suggested, laughter threading his voice as he rolled over and reached for the button fly.

Ari stopped his hand. "Let me," she said. "I can do it faster."

"That's what you think," he groaned as she propped herself up. She slipped her hand between the fabric and his abdomen, which he obligingly sucked in, and leaned over him. Working with two hands, she made quick work of the buttons.

"Don't you ever wear underwear?" Her fingertips slid over his hard length and gently freed him from the confining jeans.

"Not when I know you're coming over," he rasped. He started to sit up, as if he intended to rid himself of his jeans, but Ari pushed him down and angled her nude body against his left leg so he couldn't move.

"Uh-uh," she said, looking into Max's dark blue eyes for a second before turning away to plant kisses upon his belly while her hands still caressed him. "You're not going anywhere." Her breasts scraped along the soft denim as she lowered her head. He was big and hot against her palms, satiny smooth to the touch of her lips. She heard Max groan, then his hands grasped her upper arms. He pulled her toward him, and Ari went uncomplainingly.

Her breasts were flattened against his hard chest, and she straddled his denim-covered thigh while his tongue delved into her mouth. The power shifted as Max kept her pulled against him, refusing to slacken his grip on her arms even when she tried to take a breath. He released her mouth but kept her close. "My turn," he grasped, his voice a caress against her flushed skin as he eased her away.

Ari watched as Max slid off the bed and removed his jeans. She caught a glimpse of his strong, brown back before he leaned over her on the rumpled bed. His lips caught one nipple and tugged, sending jolts of awareness through her body. His teeth scraped her oversensitized skin as he dragged his mouth to the tip of her other breast.

When she would have reached for him he held her arms to her sides with gentle pressure and moved lower. Ari felt herself melting into him as wonderful, heated sensations engulfed her. She would have moved, but his hands continued to hold her still. When she trembled and arched against his mouth, he tightened his grip, keeping her against him until the tremors passed.

"You're mine," Max whispered as he slid above her and entered her with a smooth, filling stroke. He held himself still then, as if to give her time to memorize the feel of him, to remember the way he fitted into her snug warmth. "Say it, Arianna. Say it *now*."

Ari smoothed her hands along his broad shoulders and closed her eyes in ecstasy. "Yes."

He moved then, the rhythm strong, the motion powerful, until Ari felt the sweet, familiar pressure build and explode, leaving her slick and breathless in Max's embrace.

MUCH LATER, Max tugged Ari into the shower with him. She soaped his body until he took the bar of soap away from her and demanded equal time. Waterlogged, Ari wrapped herself in one of Max's unused bathrobes and rescued the bag of sandwiches from the living-room chair. She sat down at the kitchen table across from him, her bare feet touching his under the table while they ate the thick combination of cold cuts, vegetables, hot peppers and Italian dressing crammed into torpedo rolls. Ari took the can of beer Max handed her, and the bitter liquid cooled her mouth.

They sat outside in companionable silence and split another can of beer, watching the traffic weave along the curve of the wall, stop at the light, then continue out of sight. A group of musicians began to assemble their instruments in the gazebo across the street. Groups of people carrying folding chairs, blankets and bags of food wandered across the lawn of the town park like refugees on their way to a better land.

"This is like having ringside seats," Ari said, stretching out her bare legs on the chaise longue.

"You'd better hope the music's good, because the only way we're going to escape it is by getting in the truck and driving away."

Ari sighed in pleasure. "No, thanks. I'm happy just where I am."

"For now," Max added, a bitter tone in his voice.

"Yes," she answered, giving him a sharp look. "For now I'm very happy."

"And tomorrow? Next week? Next month?"

Tension knotted Ari's stomach, but she struggled to hide her feelings and used what she hoped would sound like a normal voice. "Tomorrow I hope to be with you. My plans next week depend on whether you're around or out on the *Million.*"

"And next month," he continued for her, "you'll be back in Bozeman, too busy to remember my name."

The band of five long-haired young men finished plugging in several miles of electrical connections and plucked a few tentative notes from their guitars. The drummer hit a few rolls.

"That's not true, and you know it. I'll be back," she said.

"When? Next summer?" The expression in his eyes was cold when he turned to look at her. "Is that supposed to be some kind of comfort?"

"Max, don't do this." Ari moved closer to touch him, but changed her mind when she saw the set of his jaw.

"What about Christmas?"

"I usually go skiing with friends. There's a resort in Jackson Hole." Her pride kept her from adding that because of him she planned to return home this year. She'd counted the days between the time she left and the day—December 15—she'd hop onto a flight home, but wasn't going to tell Max that. One hundred and twelve. "Why don't you come out and see me at Thanksgiving?"

"Never mind," he said. "I get the picture."

"Do you ski?"

"It always seemed like a waste of valuable time."

"You could come visit me before it snows."

"I have a business to run."

Ari refused to let him see how much she wanted him to come to Montana. "Haven't you ever taken a vacation, Captain Cole?"

"A few times," he admitted. "To Florida."

"You should try the Rockies," she suggested, her voice soft with promise. The leader of the band welcomed the crowd to the weekly concert, and Max shook his head. Ari knew it was no use arguing with him. Max wouldn't compromise, wouldn't change his mind. She would have to come to him—it would never be the other way around. A thick silence hung between them, broken only by the band's rendition of "I Can't Get No Satisfaction." Ari pretended to watch the enthusiastic musicians belt out the song and wondered if she should get dressed and go home.

"No promises, no regrets," Max said softly. He put his hand on her cheek. "That's what you said once, Ari. I've forgotten to play by the rules, haven't I?"

"You're allowed," she answered, ridiculously pleased to see that he wasn't angry anymore. A nagging thought wouldn't leave her alone, though. "When are you going out next?"

"First thing Monday morning."

Ari tightened the belt on her robe and stood up. She took Max's hand and tugged him inside. "Good. That means we have the next three days."

The weekend passed quicker than Ari would have dreamed possible. Neither mentioned the future again, knowing there was no reason to discuss it, no compromise to work out. Ari used her typing skills to help Max with paperwork at Cole Products. Max hauled trash from the Simone basement to the dump. At night they made love, ordered take-out food and bickered over ice-cream flavors. Before he left Sunday afternoon, Max gave her the keys to his house.

"Take it," he said, dropping the ring of keys into her palm. "Come over whenever you need the peace and quiet."

"Are you trying to make me fall in love with your house, too?"

"Of course," he said, but his blue eyes twinkled. "Actually, I was hoping you'd be waiting here for me Friday night."

"That's a distinct possibility." Ari smiled, but a fist closed around her heart at the thought of Max going out to sea again. His lips met hers before she had a chance to protest.

"HEY, AIRHEAD! It's for you!"

Ari dried her hands on a dish towel and took the phone from Joey's hand. "Hello?"

"Ari? This is Barbara Carter, Jerry's wife."

"Oh, hi!"

"Max asked me to call. He radioed in a while ago and won't be in until early tomorrow morning."

Disappointment swept over her. She'd planned dinner and seduction—not necessarily in that order—for tonight. "Well, thanks for telling me."

"I'd hoped the four of us could get together again before you left for Iowa—"

"Montana," Ari corrected, chuckling.

"Right," Barbara said. "Montana. I should've remembered—cowboys, boots, John Wayne?"

"Horses, cattle drives and prairie grass. You should see it sometime."

"I'd like that, Ari. You never know, someday we could appear on your doorstep and ask for a guided tour."

"Anytime. Does Jerry take the *Million* out Sunday?"

"Or Monday." Ari heard a note of worry in Barbara's voice. "Right now he's in bed with the stomach flu. If he isn't better by tomorrow night, I'll have to take him to a doctor."

"The poor man—is there anything I can do?"

"No," Barb said, her voice cheerful again. "He's pretty tough. I'm sure he'll be fine tomorrow. Oh, I heard Coe's wife had twins. Boys or girls?"

"Girls. We're all thrilled, and they're due to come home from the hospital next week."

"Congratulate Coe and his wife for me, will you?"

"Sure. And tell Jerry I hope he feels better."

Ari hung up the phone, wishing she'd had a chance to get to know Barbara better. The blond woman's friendliness had been an unexpected pleasure last month after the near fiasco at the wedding. Ari felt unsettled. She'd be leaving in ten days, yet didn't feel as if she'd accomplished anything this summer. Her parents' house was a lot closer to being empty, but they hadn't shown much interest in moving into their new home.

And she'd made the ridiculous mistake of falling in love with a man who wanted her—not to mention their life together—on his own terms.

The good news was she'd peeled a lot of potatoes—the blisters on her thumb attested to that—thereby contributing to several hundred gallons of clam chowder and consequently increasing her mother's new furniture bank account. Peggy had her eye on a brown velour couch.

Ten days until summer was a thing of the past. Ari willed herself not to think about it anymore. Tonight, or tomorrow morning, Max would return. She'd be waiting in his house, maybe even in his bed—shamelessly—but when there were only ten days left to love the man she loved, there was no sense in letting false pride or modesty get in the way.

11

"ARI?"

The word was a soft whisper near her ear. Ari lifted a hand to brush it away.

"Want to go to the beach?"

Her fingertips connected with freshly shaven skin before her hand dropped back to her cheek. "What?" she mumbled, burrowing deeper into the pillows.

"It's after nine. I thought we could spend the day at the beach."

"What?"

"Beach," Max answered, smoothing the tangle of dark curls from Ari's face. "Sand. Water. High tide. Sea gulls. Remember?"

As the words penetrated her fuzzy brain, Ari stretched and struggled to open her eyes. She rolled onto her back and met Max's amused expression. "Hey, you're home!"

Max nodded. "And you're in my bed. I like that."

"I tried to stay awake, but I guess it didn't work."

"You don't look like you're awake now." He eased himself from the mattress. His white T-shirt accentuated his tan, and Ari caught a glimpse of black bathing trunks. "There's a pot of coffee downstairs. I'll pack a lunch, then we can swing by your house and get your bathing suit."

Ari tried to sit up. "You don't have to. I brought it with me because I went swimming last night. Look, Max—"

But he was already in the doorway. "Humor me, sweetheart. It was a long haul and I need to feel land under me again."

"All right," she promised. "I'll hurry." Ari did move quickly, wanting her morning dose of caffeine more than she wanted to go to the beach. Blue sky filled the bedroom window. It was one of those hot, bright August days that made Rhode Islanders flock to the shore. Her yellow suit had dried, draped over a rod in the other bathroom, so she tugged it on and pulled her coral sundress over her head. Then she brushed her teeth and fixed her hair by pulling it into a loose ponytail.

When she appeared in the kitchen Max was loading the dishwasher. "Want something to eat?"

"No, thanks," she said, pouring coffee into the red mug waiting by the coffeepot. She took a dip and noticed that an open blue-and-white cooler sat in front of the refrigerator. She peeked inside at the array of plastic-wrapped sandwiches and fresh fruit. "I'll wait." Max shut the dishwasher door and wiped his hands on a paper towel. He looked pleased with himself. "You've been to the grocery store already."

"Yeah. I like waking up beside you," he said.

"I'm sorry I didn't hear you come home."

"The light was on and you were still holding your book."

"The story of my life," she muttered, taking another swallow of coffee.

"Speaking of your life," Max went on, leaning against the counter while he watched her, "why don't you spend the rest of it right here?"

"Don't tease me." His words upset Ari and she tried to hide her dismay. He'd asked her to stay in Rhode Island, but she didn't want to hear it. Staying with Max would be heaven when he was home and hell when he was out fishing.

"That's right," he said, looking away. "I forgot—you haven't had ten cups of coffee to make you civilized. Here," he added, pouring the rest of the pot of coffee into a multicolored plastic thermos. "Take it with you."

THEY SPREAD THEIR BLANKET a few yards from the water and anchored the corners with towels and shoes. Ari was content to sip her coffee and let the warmth of the morning sun soak into her skin while she waited to wake up. She and Max sat contentedly watching people arrive at the beach and stake out their square of sand with blankets, chairs and umbrellas.

Max finally broke the companionable silence. "When do you have to leave?"

"I have reservations for August 27."

"What day is that?"

"A Monday."

He looked at the horizon for a long moment. "This is the eighteenth already. I'll be working at the plant this week and probably won't have to leave again until after then."

"Okay."

"Ari, take some time this week to think about staying here with me."

She'd probably think about nothing else, Ari knew, but it wouldn't change the outcome. "Thinking about it isn't going to change anything."

"You never know." He flashed her a grin. "I might charm you yet."

Ari leaned back on her elbows and pretended to watch the small waves roll in. "You overestimate your powers."

"I got you aboard the Block Island boat, didn't I?" At her nod he continued. "I suppose I could always kidnap you again, make you miss your flight."

"And keep me barefoot and pregnant, your captive on the island?"

He pretended to consider it. "Doesn't sound too bad, does it?"

"I guess if there was enough to read, I wouldn't mind too much."

"You need your own bookstore."

She chuckled, relieved to change the direction of the conversation. "Maybe I should have been a librarian, but I'd rather read the books than catalog them."

"And you like teaching." It wasn't a question.

"Of course. Do you wish I didn't?"

"Yes," he said. "It would make things much easier."

"Easier for whom?"

Max didn't answer, except to ask if she wanted lunch.

Later they held hands and ambled along the sand.

"Stay here," Max told her. He gripped her hand tightly and they walked the length of the beach while an inch of water lapped at their ankles. He negotiated a tricky bypass of a child's sand castle and surrounding moat without letting go of Ari's hand.

"I can't."

"You won't, you mean."

"What do you want, Max?"

"I want you to marry me."

Ari's heart stopped briefly at his bald statement. "I can't."

They walked in silence for a few minutes, amid shrieking toddlers, splashing swimmers and the calls of teenage boys tossing a Frisbee into the shallow water.

"Do you love me?"

"Yes," she said and sighed. "But that doesn't change things, Max."

"We'd have a good life."

"I'd have to give up everything. Would you stop going out to sea?"

"That's my life, Ari, my business."

"Cole Products is your business, too."

"A struggling one," he admitted.

"I can't live worrying and waiting for the rest of my life. I've seen the look on my mother's face when the storm warnings were posted and Dad wasn't home yet. I've already lost someone I loved, Max."

"You won't lose me."

"There are no guarantees, Max."

"There are no guarantees I won't be hit by a car, crossing the street on the way home this afternoon, either."

"No, but what happens? I give up my job—"

Max stopped her, turning her to face him. "There are other jobs. Why don't you teach at the University of Rhode Island?"

"It's not that simple." She looked into his warm blue eyes and wished it were as easy as he thought it could be.

"Yes, it is. It's as simple as my loving you and you loving me. If we concentrate on that everything else will fall into place."

"It will fall into place because I'll fall into place, won't it?" Ari knew Max would never compromise, not when it meant giving up what he loved to do.

"That's not true."

"It isn't?" She felt sad and tired and lonely just thinking about being a couple of thousand miles away from him, but she wasn't going to put herself through the pain of losing him, or through the torment of dealing with his life-style.

"Other women are married to guys like me."

"You don't think they worry?" She stopped and looked up at him incredulously. "There are enough widow's walks on top of houses in this state to give us all the creeps. And you know why they call them that, don't you?"

"Ari—"

She cut off his words, knowing he wasn't going to give her an answer. "Because the women standing on them to watch for their husbands' return from the sea didn't know they were already widows. That their men were never coming home."

They walked to the end of the beach. A strand of seaweed knotted around Ari's ankle and she kicked it aside.

"I love you. It's not going to change."

"Max..."

He stopped and bent to pick something out of the smooth sand and Ari watched curiously. Kevin had found a diamond ring sticking out of the sand the summer he was twelve, and her parents still loved to tell the story of how he had tried to give it to a neighborhood girl he'd wanted to impress.

"Here." Max held out his palm and showed her a piece of green glass. Opaque green, it had been tossed by the sand and waves until its originally sharp edges were round and smooth to the touch.

"Beach glass," she said. "My grandmother used to collect it."

"The green is probably from an old Coca-Cola bottle someone tossed overboard years ago." He took her hand and placed the bit of glass, no bigger than a nickel, into her palm. "Someone's trash turned into something beautiful and worth collecting. Amazing, isn't it?"

"What's amazing?"

"How time changes things."

"Are you talking about us now?"

He nodded, the grooves in his face etched deep as he examined her. "You could give us time, Ari. Time to make this work between us."

There didn't seem to be anything left to say. Everything had changed with his proposal—because he wanted it all his own way, refusing to consider that he might have to change, too.

"I can give you anything you want, Ari," he went on, closing her fingers over the glass. "My home, my love, my heart." His deep blue eyes held her gaze. "I can't give you my life, though, and the sea is all I know and all I've ever known. My father left me a boat—he died from a heart attack when I was sixteen—and a run-down third-rate packing plant. I've made my own way ever since. My mother remarried and took my sisters with her to Boston, but I stayed here and did what I could with what my father taught me. It's all I had then and it's all I have now."

"That's not true."

"Look at me, Ari. I'm Max Cole, a fisherman. All the fancy electronic equipment and new boats and expensive town houses won't change that. You have to take me as I am or not at all." She started to hand the piece of glass back to him. "No," he growled, "you keep it. Call it a good-luck charm. Call it a reminder of...what did you call it that night in Newport?"

"The last great affair," she whispered.

"Yeah." His voice was bitter. "The last great affair. Just remember, I was willing to make it a hell of a lot more than that."

It wasn't something she was likely to forget, Ari thought ruefully. They declared a silent, uneasy truce as they walked back to their blanket. The day seemed spoiled now, and even the cold apple she bit into didn't lift her spirits.

"I'll be back next summer." She wanted to stroke his back, feel the heat absorbed by his skin.

"I don't want another summer romance, Ari. I'm not going to spend the rest of my life this way."

"All right." She had no idea why she was saying that when clearly nothing was right at all. "You won't have to." Ari took a shaky breath. "It's over."

"UNITED FLIGHT 281 to Chicago now boarding. All passengers proceed to the security gate. Repeat, United Flight 281 to Chicago now boarding."

Ari slung her tote bag over her shoulder as she turned to say goodbye to her parents. Peggy dabbed at her eyes with a handkerchief and Rusty looked as if he wanted to burst into tears along with his wife. "Come on, Mom," Ari begged, her voice rough. "You're going to visit me soon, right? Didn't you promise?"

Peggy nodded, too choked up to speak.

"Damn it, I hate airports," Rusty said, enfolding his daughter in his arms.

"I never—" Peggy wept "—*never* thought you'd leave this time. What is the captain going to say?"

He'd had plenty of time in the past ten days to say anything he wanted, Ari thought. The silence had been cruel, but understandable. She managed her best stiff-upper-lip imitation. "He knew the day I had to leave, Mother."

"Last I heard the *Million* was off Tom's Canyon," Rusty pointed out. "Don't know if they were in any fish or not, though."

"I'd better go," Ari said, hoping she could keep a grip on her emotions until her parents were out of sight.

"You don't want us to wait at the gate with you?"

Ari shook her head. "Love you," was all she could manage when she turned away. The lump in her throat grew to baseball size as she squeezed through the crowded lobby of Green Airport. She stood in line at the security counter and then, once through without a problem, hesitated, looking through the glass wall hoping for a glimpse of a tall, dark-haired man with sea-blue eyes. She wished he'd come to say goodbye, but didn't know how she would have reacted if he had. *It's better this way. A clean break, a quick getaway.*

Still, Ari stood watching the airport lobby until the last call to board the plane.

SHE'S GONE. FINALLY. Max stood behind the *Lady Million*'s wheelhouse and looked down on the pile of fish ready to be either returned to the sea or sorted by the crew. He paid no attention to the loud cries of scavenging sea gulls, the slapping tails of tons of dying fish or to the monotonous hum of the *Million*'s 835-horsepower engine. *She's gone* screeched through his head. It was not unlike the sound of the hydraulic winch that hauled in the net hour after hour.

He could have been home, might have been able to stop her, if only Jerry hadn't had to have his appendix out.... No, that wasn't necessarily true. The woman had made it clear from the very first day: no commitments, no fishermen. She'd made her choice; he'd made his. That had to be the end of it.

Max moved back into the shelter of the wheelhouse, unable to avoid the diesel's sickening fumes. He shoved his hands into the pockets of his oilskin jacket and prayed the pain would go away quickly.

THE TWO-HOUR time difference took a little getting used to. Ari rose earlier, craved lunch at ten and by evening had started yawning before nine-thirty. Her days were long, filled with department meetings, paperwork, planning the changes in the year's classes, ironing out the hassles in the schedule and catching up with friends.

Throughout the fall she told no one about Maximilian Cole. She thought it would be easier to hold the broken pieces of her heart together without an audience, without anyone's sympathy disrupting the shaky healing process she had to go through. Ari had no time to admire the distant Rockies. The clear, chilly Montana mornings raised goose bumps on her arms as she walked to her office, and the wide starry sky did little to help her sleep when she finally climbed into her bed each night. In her wildest dreams she'd never imagined it would hurt this much.

THE TELEPHONE RANG as Ari finished handing out Halloween treats to a tiny pink rabbit, a monster, a skeleton and a sophisticatedly made-up punk rocker. It was a school night, and the children had begun ringing doorbells as soon as dusk fell.

"You're welcome!" she called one final time before crossing the tiny living room to the couch. She'd tossed the portable phone onto one of the cushions after her last conversation.

"Hello?"

"Ari," Peggy said. "Thank God."

"What's wrong?" Ice settled in her stomach as she waited for her mother to answer. *"What?"*

"It's Max, honey. I thought you should know—"

"Know *what?*"

Rusty's voice came through on the extension. "Now, honey—"

Peg's words were hurried. "There's been a bad storm, and the *Lady Million's* missing."

"And Max?"

"Was on board. With Jerry."

"How long?"

"Two days," her father answered. "But there's still hope. Both boys are good sailors and know what they're doing."

Ari knew that didn't always guarantee survival. It was the only comfort her father could give though, and she recognized the meager hope his words offered. "Yes," she said, crumpling to the couch. "Max always knows what he's doing."

"We thought you should know." Meaning *we thought you should be prepared*, Ari knew. Peggy's voice sounded far away, and Ari knew her mother was crying and trying to muffle the sound. "Those boys need all the prayers they can get," she said.

"I feel so helpless."

"We all do, hon." Rusty's voice cracked. "There's nothing left to do but—like your mother said—pray for the boys' safe homecoming."

"You'll call me right away if there's any . . . news?"

"We sure will," Rusty said. "We've got the scanner on all the time."

Ari put the phone down as the doorbell chimed once again. This time she didn't hurry to answer it, struggling instead to rise from the couch. Her legs felt as if they were weighted with sandbags. She passed out candy bars for the next hour and a half, hoping the excited neighborhood children wouldn't notice her artificial smile and trembling hands.

Then, when the children had finished celebrating Halloween, Ari took the portable phone to bed with her and told the friends who called that there'd been a family emergency. She refused all offers to keep her company, choosing instead to curl up in her bed, uncorrected English papers stacked beside her, the phone an inch away from her on the mattress.

She couldn't imagine Max dead. She couldn't allow herself to think that Max, Jerry and the crew of the *Lady Million* had gone to their deaths in the murky ocean in the middle of nowhere. She didn't cry, didn't eat, didn't move from the bed except to fix pots of mint tea and go to the bathroom. She didn't look at herself in the mirror, afraid the truth would stare back at her and she would have to face the painful reality of another loss.

He couldn't be dead. Not Max. Not Maximilian Cole, with the crinkling blue eyes, the laugh lines etched round his mouth, the strong body that meshed so beautifully with hers when they made love. The vibrant man who loved chocolate ice cream, rare steak and walking on the beach couldn't possibly be dead.

Finally she opened her dresser drawer and unwrapped a piece of cotton tucked deep in the corner of her jewelry box. The beach glass stared back at her. She picked it up and gripped it tightly in her hand. *I love you, Max. Do you know that? Be safe, be well, come home.* The words were the only prayer she could think of.

Ari mercilessly graded papers until dawn, then switched from tea to coffee until it was time to get ready. Thursdays were her light days, with classes at ten and two, staff meetings at four. She tucked the piece of glass into the pocket of her corduroy jumper before venturing outside, hating to leave the telephone, but knowing her mother had her office number. She wanted to call home, but stopped before dialing. She couldn't hear their voices again, not right before going to work. She climbed into her little sedan and drove the three chilly miles to the university, worrying about Barbara, praying that the crew of the *Lady Million* would be safe and sound and hauling back to Point Judith as secure and intact as when she'd left the harbor.

The day passed with agonizing slowness. Ari prepared to fly home, wanting the soft comfort of her mother's arms wrapped around her. The faculty meeting dragged on past five o'clock, adjourned for drinks at a nearby restaurant. Numb with worry and exhaustion, Ari pleaded a headache and drove home to her silent apartment.

The light blinked on her answering machine, but before Ari could hear the messages she fixed herself a stiff rum and Coke, turned up the thermostat to 74° and exchanged her shoes for scruffy bedroom slippers. She sat down on the sofa and finished the drink before she flicked the switch to hear her messages.

"Honey, it's Mom. Are you there?" A second's pause. "There's no news yet, but the coast guard is still looking. I'll call you later." Beep.

Ari listened to the rest of the messages—all local, not important—and wished she had the courage to call home.

She couldn't bear it happening all over again. She wanted to go home. Maybe if she was there she could change it and make it all come out okay. As if the sheer force of her willpower would bring the boat home safely. *There's been a bad storm....*

She'd heard the words before.

This morning she'd bought a newspaper and read about the high winds along the East coast from New York to Maine. She'd looked at the weather map and studied the signs. She could probably turn on the national news and be shown pictures of another near hurricane in the Atlantic, but didn't want to see for herself how bad it had been.

The phone rang, long and shrill, before Ari pounced on it. "Hello?"

"Hi, honey."

Ari gripped the telephone tightly between her two hands and held it tightly against her ear. "Mom?"

"It's okay. They're all safe."

Relief swept through her, bringing an incoming tide of tears that welled into her eyes and overflowed down her cheeks. "They're . . . home?"

"Not yet. They were blown off course, found in Canadian waters. It's taken the Canadian officials a while to contact the coast guard, because they were hit with the storm after it went through here."

Noisy sobs shook Ari, much to her embarrassment. She knew her parents would worry about her, and it would break her father's heart to hear her cry on the phone. "Sorry," was all she could get out.

"That's all right, Ari, you just let it out. Lord knows what hell you've been through today."

"I was going to fly home." *For the funeral.*

"Well, you still can," Peggy said, her voice brightening.

"No." Ari took a shaky breath. "That wouldn't be a very good idea."

"We're moving into the house next weekend," Rusty told her. "In time for the holidays. Russ and Karen will have a few weeks to get settled before Thanksgiving."

"And," Peggy chimed in, "I bought that new brown sofa I told you about."

"That's great." *Max is safe.*

"We're keeping the old phone number, you know."

"And I'm taking your mother to Florida right after New Year's."

"That's great," Ari repeated, feeling as if she were listening to her father's voice from the end of a tunnel. *Max is safe.*

"You get some rest, Ari. You think about coming home for Christmas. Those new baby girls need to see their godmother, you know."

"Okay, Mom. I'll try. Bye."

"Ari?"

"What, Mom?"

"You want me to give any message to the captain? I could tell him to call you," Peggy suggested hopefully.

"No, that's okay. I'll, uh, get in touch with him in a couple of weeks."

Peggy didn't argue. Ari hung up the phone and replaced it on its holder in the kitchen. She'd been right to come back to Montana, right to avoid loving a sea captain. She'd known all along about the pain such a love would cause; she'd been right to turn away from Max and come home to the Rockies.

But, a logical little voice inside piped up, *you've been suffering anyway, haven't you?*

Not anymore.

Always, the voice insisted.

Ari paced around her tiny apartment, finally collapsing onto the unmade bed. She fell into a deep sleep and dreamed of waves and wind, ocean storms with purple winds billowing like sheets across Max's smiling face. Of course he was happy, because piles of goldfish lay on the deck of his little rowboat and a voluptuous mermaid and her kitten were curled at Max's bare feet.

"HAPPY THANKSGIVING!"

"Same to you, Ruthie. How are the girls?"

"Beautiful. Getting bigger every day."

"Thanks for the pictures. I have them framed on my desk. How's Coe?" It was a typical marathon phone call, Simone style. Two extensions, a different voice every ninety seconds, and chaos providing background noise.

"He's standing right here. Wait a sec."

"Hey, Ari!" Coe's voice rang through the receiver. "You watching the game?"

"One of them," Ari said. "I'm not sure which one, though. How's everything with you, besides with the twins?"

"Great. I've picked up a couple of construction jobs—inside work—so that helps. I saw your friend down at the Pier the other day." His voice became distant. "Wait, Ruthie, will ya?"

"What friend?"

"Max Cole, your old boyfriend. I waved but I don't think he saw me. He was busy helping someone walk her dogs."

Max was involved with the veterinarian's assistant? "Oh, well . . ." Ari struggled for something to say. "That's nice."

"Yeah. He had about five of them on a leash—all right, Ruth. I'm coming. Bye, Ari," he called, then handed the phone to someone else.

Ari spoke to her brothers, her sisters-in-law and a couple of her nephews before Peggy took over the telephone.

"Where are you calling from?"

"The old house. Karen's going to start painting soon. She has a lot of plans, so I'm glad they're happy with the place."

"And what about you? You like the new house?"

"Oh, I'm just as happy as a clam at high tide. Your father and I—oops, wait a minute." Ari heard some muffled shouts before her mother returned to the phone. "One of the little ones took off with the carving knife. It's a miracle no one got hurt. When are you going out? Are the roads bad?"

"Pretty soon," Ari replied. "It's always a nice day at Minna's, and everyone brings their favorite Thanksgiving dish. We have a few feet of snow on the ground, but the roads are clear."

"Well, I'm glad you're not going to be alone."

"I've been going to Minna's for eight years, Mom. It's like family." She heard loud cheers in the background.

"A touchdown," Peggy explained.

"I heard."

"What about Christmas? You're coming home, aren't you?"

"I don't know yet, Mom."

"Well, if it's money—"

"It's not. I'll let you know next week."

"All right." Peggy sighed. "You let me know."

"I promise."

"There's an article about Max in *The Narragansett Times*. You want me to send it?"

"Sure," Ari said, hoping she sounded casual. She didn't know if she really wanted to know any more about Max's business. "What's it about?"

"It's mostly an article on the packing plant. Max is going to Japan sometime this month to learn their way of packaging seafood and fish."

"Well, good for him." At least he wouldn't be walking dogs.

"Wait, here's your father. Bye, honey."

"Bye," Ari responded, but her mother had already passed the phone to Rusty.

"Ari?"

"Hi, Dad."

"You snowed in up there?"

"Nope. I'm just fine." She chatted with her father for a few minutes—he was always vitally interested in Bozeman's windchill temperatures—and then hung up the phone. Ari wished she was right there in the middle of the festivities instead of alone, letting the football game on television fill the apartment with sound.

Christmas in Rhode Island sounded more tempting all the time. After all, she wanted to see her parents settled in their new house, hear Karen's plans for the rambling old one, and hold the twins. It would be fun to watch her rowdy nephews open their presents in person for a change.

She wouldn't necessarily run into Max just because they were in the same state. She wouldn't have to call him, drop by his office to bring him a fruitcake or sing Christmas carols at his front door. She wouldn't have to see him at all, if she didn't want to. She'd had her chance for a life with Maximilian Cole, and she'd turned it down.

And if, by some wild coincidence, she should encounter him at the movies or along the seawall, she could probably manage not to fall at his feet and beg him to take her home, make love to her and never go to sea again. She could probably manage that with no trouble at all—right after she picked up the Rocky Mountains and moved them into Mississippi.

12

"THIS PRESENT came for you," Peggy said, handing Ari a brightly wrapped package. "Be careful, it's heavy."

Ari took the box and looked for a card. Nothing but her name decorated the glitter-edged tag. "I can't open a gift nine days before Christmas."

"Sure you can." Peggy nodded. "It says so."

Sure enough, Open before Christmas was scrawled on the side. Very mysterious, Ari thought, then wondered if jet lag had fuddled her mind. She'd been delayed five hours at O'Hare while crews worked to plow the runways. She'd been up since five and traveling for the past nineteen hours. She even smelled like an airplane. "I'll wait," she said, putting the heavy box back into its place under the tree. "The house looks wonderful."

"We like it," Rusty said.

"See the couch, Ari? It looks nice with the curtains, doesn't it?"

Ari nodded, and her father patted her shoulder. "Tomorrow I'll show you my shop out in the garage. The boys gave me an early Christmas present, a radial-arm saw, so I've been practicing to make the little girls rocking horses."

Ari explored the tiny two-bedroom ranch house with her mother and together they unpacked Ari's suitcases, one of which was filled with presents. "I couldn't bring much, so I thought I'd spend the rest of the week finishing up my Christmas shopping." She glanced out the window at the fat flakes of snow drifting past the glass. "That is, if we don't have a big storm tonight."

"Well, your plane made it in okay. That's what matters." Peggy patted Ari's face. "You look too thin. Want me to make you a sandwich? Did you eat on the plane? Was it good?"

"No, yes, no, but thanks anyway. I think I'd rather take a shower before I make any—"

"Fine," her mother said. "Go make yourself beautiful."

"I don't want to work that hard," Ari protested with a chuckle. "I just want to get out of these clothes and into something that doesn't smell like I've worn it for the past twenty hours."

"Fine," Peggy said again, shooing Ari toward the bathroom. "I'll make some tea, then you can open your present."

Twenty minutes later, Ari sat down on the new couch with the mysterious box in front of her on the coffee table. "You really think I should open it?"

Rusty rolled his eyes toward the ceiling and shrugged. "Give up, Peg. If the girl doesn't want to open it, you can't make her." He turned to his daughter. "Drink your tea, honey. That present's been sitting under the tree for three days—I guess it can sit a little longer."

"Did someone deliver it?"

Peggy frowned. "I found it on the doorstep. That's all I know. You don't want a present? So, don't open a present."

"Now you're making me crazy," Ari remarked, plucking the silver bow from the top of the box. She stripped the paper and popped the tape from the lid.

Peg and Rusty leaned forward in their matching recliners.

"Well?"

"Just a minute, Mom. There are about a hundred of those foam peanuts in here. You don't want them all over the floor, do you?"

"Why should I care? What's in the box?"

Packing material spilled over Ari's lap as she lifted a glass jar from the box. From the small imperfections in the glass Ari guessed that it was a very old container. But it was the contents that took her breath away, for inside were hundreds of pieces of beach glass. Green, white and an occasional rare blue piece filled the old-fashioned apothecary jar.

"Looks like an old candy jar," Rusty commented. "How about that?"

Ari lifted the lid and reached in to touch the beach glass. The faintest smell of sea greeted her as she let the bits of smooth glass trail through her fingers. A few months ago Max had tucked a piece of glass into her hand. *You could give us time, Ari. Time to make things work between us.*

But she hadn't given them the time. She'd run off, instead of standing still to face her fears.

"Who sent her that?" Rusty asked Peg.

"She knows."

Ari looked up at both of them. "Max must have. I don't know how to explain it."

"You don't have to," Peg told her. "He's outside, waiting for you on the deck. I only hope the poor man hasn't frozen to death in the snow."

Rusty looked confused. "What the hell is a grown man doing on the deck?"

Peggy winked at her husband as Ari flew off the couch, scattering packing material in every direction. "I called him."

"Then why in God's name didn't he knock?"

Ari groped for the switch by the kitchen door and managed to flood the backyard with light before seeing Max's broad outline. She opened the door and stepped into the cold night, unwilling to wait for Max to come inside to touch him.

"Max?" She stopped before rushing headlong into his arms. He was bundled up in a thick navy parka, his head was bare and snow dusted his dark hair. She couldn't read the expression in his eyes.

"You opened it?"

Ari nodded. She couldn't tell if he was pleased or not. "I was supposed to, wasn't I?"

"Yes, of course." He held out his hand and Ari stepped forward and placed hers inside.

"I love it." Ari wanted to weep at the feeling of touching him again.

"Come on," he said, tugging her toward the steps. "You're going with me."

"Max—" Ari started to protest. "Come inside."

"No. This time you're going to give me time to say everything that needs to be said."

"I'm in my robe, for heaven's sake." The chill was beginning to seep through the rubber soles of Ari's slippers. "And I don't have boots on."

Max picked her up easily and held her in his arms. "There. Now your feet won't get wet."

"I'm freezing." She wrapped her arms around his neck, but his jacket, damp with snow, provided little warmth.

"So am I. But I'll have the heater in the truck going in just a minute."

"We're not getting on the Block Island boat, are we?"

"I thought of it." He smiled down at Ari and the tightness around her heart eased. "But it's faster to my place."

"What about my parents? They think I'm outside with you."

"Peg knows where we're going. She also knows why."

"And I don't."

"You will in a few minutes." He set her down on the pavement while he opened the truck door, then helped her climb in. Ari was ridiculously glad she'd worn her new robe—an apricot quilted satin with lace lapels. The gown underneath wasn't too shabby either, bought for hanging around the house on Christmas morning.

"Nice color," he said when the interior lights popped on, illuminating the inside of the truck. He started the engine and drove silently to the Pier. Ari sat and looked out the window at the snow that hit the windshield. She wanted to believe that everything was going to be all right, but didn't dare.

After he parked, Max swept her up into his arms once more, carrying her to the stairway that was protected from the weather before setting her down a second time. When Ari stepped into the living room, she felt as if she was coming home. Max took her into his arms and held her tightly, so tightly she could barely breathe. She clung to him, wondering if she could put into words how she felt, knowing he was safe. "I was so worried," she whispered against his jacket.

"I promised myself that if we—and the *Million*—made it back home in one piece, I'd go after you," Max whispered. "I would bring you back here and make you stay."

She pulled away and looked into his dark eyes. "You can't make me stay, Max."

"I know." His voice was sad. "But I can make love to you."

"That won't solve anything."

He smiled. "It will warm us up."

She couldn't resist him and didn't particularly want to try. "You have a point."

"Come on, then," he said, wrapping one arm around her shoulder and heading toward the stairs. "I have a surprise for you."

"How did you know I was coming home?"

"Your mother is an endless supply of information."

"Figures," Ari muttered as Max opened the bedroom door. A brightly lit Christmas tree stood in the corner opposite the bed. Other than the blinking colors from the tree, the room was dark.

"Provides atmosphere, don't you think?"

"I love it," she said, stepping over to inhale the fragrant pine scent. "You did this yourself?"

He unzipped his jacket and tossed it on a chair. "Why wouldn't I?"

"I don't know." She shrugged. "I hear you've been walking dogs."

He grimaced. "Yeah. I tried to pretend your leaving didn't hurt. That didn't work."

"It's all right—I just wondered." She paused, fingering the pine needles. "Did you answer any more of the letters?"

"Yes."

She spun around to face him. *"Yes?"*

Max ran his hands down the silky fabric, caressing Ari's shoulders. "I answered every single one and told them I was no longer available."

"Why?"

"Because there's only one woman I want to kidnap. Even if she does prefer cowboys."

"She hasn't seen any cowboys in a long, long time. And she's not running away anymore, ever again."

His lips brushed hers, starting the familiar, tantalizing heat. Moments later he untied the belt at her waist and eased the robe from her shoulders. His fingers grazed the lace collar of the silky nightgown before lifting her chin. He gazed into her warm brown eyes. "Are you ever going to marry me?"

"I've thought about it a lot in the past weeks."

"And?"

"You scared me to death, Max. I thought I'd never see you again."

He hated seeing the moisture well up in her eyes. "I'll never do that to you again, sweetheart. I promise."

She shook her head, forcing him to take his hand away from her face. "You can't. It's part of your life and I have to accept that."

"No."

"No?" Ari stared at him, waiting for an explanation.

"I've made some choices, too. Barbara's pregnant— she came close to having a miscarriage when our boat was lost. Jerry and I realized how close we came to losing everything, and we decided to sell the *Million* and invest more time and money into the packing plant. I'd also like to get involved in protecting the breeding grounds so there'll be plenty of fish to go around in years to come. Sounds crazy?"

She shook her head. "Sounds great."

"Will you mind living here?"

"No." Ari thought of the beautiful snow-covered mountains she'd left behind. "But I know where we'll spend our vacations."

He grinned. "I may turn into one of the those Sunday fishermen, though."

"Good," she said. "You can teach the boys how to fish."

Max looked confused. "Your brothers?"

She wrapped her arms around his waist and smiled up at him. "Your sons."

Epilogue

JERRY CARTER WATCHED his best friend pace back and forth across the tiled floor of the chancel. "Kind of brings it all back, doesn't it?"

Max frowned, shoved his hands into the pockets of his white pants and continued marching up and down. "Are you sure you haven't seen her come in?"

"Well, let me see," Jerry drawled, stepping to peer around the door frame. "Nope, nothing yet. The church is pretty crowded, though."

Max glanced at his watch. "Five minutes after twelve. She's late. She's never late."

"I love June weddings, don't you?" A baby's wail pierced the hum of the crowd seated in the sanctuary beyond. "Uh-oh. That cry sounds familiar."

Max almost smiled. "I hope you told my godson to behave himself."

"Barbara's nursing him every five minutes, so he'll be fine. It's you I'm worried about. In a few minutes, Ari is going to walk down that aisle." The organ music stopped and the priest gestured to the two men to join him on the steps of the altar. Jerry continued his running monologue. "That's why we're all here today, to see you joined in holy wedlock."

"For heaven's sake, will you shut up?" Max didn't take his gaze off the aisle as the music started once again and the bridesmaids, elegantly dressed in shades of peach and white, stepped gracefully past the pews.

The music shifted once again, and the guests stood to greet the bride. Max thought his heart would burst as Ari, her arm tucked through Rusty's, appeared in the doorway. A familiar wide brim—Max's gift to his bride—shaded Ari's skin from the sunshine that peeked through the stained glass windows and highlighted her Victorian, high-necked gown.

Jerry poked him in the ribs. "Is that her?"

Apricot ribbons streamed from the bouquet of white roses in Ari's hand, and tendrils of dark curls brushed against her flushed cheeks. She was the most beautiful woman he'd ever seen, and Max wondered nervously if he'd be able to swallow the lump in his throat to speak when the time came to say, "I do."

He took a deep breath and missed Rusty's teary wink. "Yes," he said with a gulp. "That's her. She's the one wearing the white hat."

Harlequin Intrigue

QUID PRO QUO

Racketeer King Crawley is a man who lives by one rule: An Eye For An Eye. Put behind bars for his sins against humanity, Crawley is driven by an insatiable need to get even with the judge who betrayed him. And the only way to have his revenge is for the judge's children to suffer for their father's sins....

Harlequin Intrigue introduces Patricia Rosemoor's QUID PRO QUO series: #161 PUSHED TO THE LIMIT (May 1991), #163 SQUARING ACCOUNTS (June 1991) and #165 NO HOLDS BARRED (July 1991).

Meet:

Sydney Raferty: She is the first to feel the wrath of King Crawley's vengeance. Pushed to the brink of insanity, she must fight her way back to reality—with the help of Benno DeMartino in #161 PUSHED TO THE LIMIT.

Dakota Raferty: The judge's only son, he is a man whose honest nature falls prey to the racketeer's madness. With Honor Bright, he becomes an unsuspecting pawn in a game of deadly revenge in #163 SQUARING ACCOUNTS.

Asia Raferty: The youngest of the siblings, she is stalked by Crawley and must find a way to end the vendetta. Only one man can help—Dominic Crawley. But will the son join forces with his father's enemy in #165 NO HOLDS BARRED?

Don't miss a single title of Patricia Rosemoor's QUID PRO QUO trilogy coming to you from Harlequin Intrigue.

Back by Popular Demand

Janet Dailey
Americana

A romantic tour of America through fifty favorite Harlequin Presents® novels, each set in a different state researched by Janet and her husband, Bill. A journey of a lifetime in one cherished collection.

In June, don't miss the sultry states featured in:

Title # 9 - FLORIDA
        Southern Nights
   #10 - GEORGIA
        Night of the Cotillion

Available wherever Harlequin books are sold.

JD-JR